NEVER MINE

TARANNUM BOSE

TRUE SIGN
PUBLISHING HOUSE

Published by True Sign Publishing House
Address: SY. No. 21/2 & 21/3, Sonnenahalli,
Krishnarajapura, Bengaluru,
Karnataka - 560049 India
E-mail: truesignbooks@gmail.com
Website: www.truesign.in

Never Mine

Author: Tarannum Bose

ISBN: 978-93-5584-981-6

First Edition: 2023

NEVER MINE

Shanaya tries to swallow the lump of bitterness in her throat at the thought of Sidharth. Holding her favorite photograph of them in her hands, she stops herself from crying again. She has clearly touched it several times with tears stained on it. You can still distinguish the big smiles on their faces if you just look at it closely. Sometimes we just don't know the value of a moment until it becomes a memory. And sometimes, these happiest memories hurt you the most.

Shanaya loved photographs because they were proof of how even once, maybe just for a heartbeat, everything was perfect, but a lot of things can change in a year. Shanaya and Sidharth did too.

Maybe if only love was as easy as it's easy to spell, then maybe It would not break hundreds of relationships in a single minute every day. And maybe, just maybe, Shanaya could have saved her own as well. The only relationship which meant the most to her, but for saving it, she stood motionless.

It was Monday. The day Shanaya hated the most after pulling an all-nighter. She took a glance at her class schedule, which was shitty, 3 hours of lecture and it starts at 7 in the morning. She didn't get the best sleep the previous night and woke up late, so she skipped breakfast. Reason #545 Why she hates her life so much.

She was in between her short mandatory nap session when she could hear noises in her sleep.

"Hi." The brown- haired boy greets Shanaya softly and takes a seat beside her.

Shanaya just looks at him boringly. She was exhausted and her best friend was not helping her.

"Is this the photography class? I was absent yesterday, so I'm not sure."

"Sid, my head hurts terrible, stop making bad jokes." Shanaya rolled her eyes and rested her head on her arms on the table. She tries to go back to sleep, as Sidharth laughs loudly at his own antics with annoying Shanaya.

"Cranky much?" Sidharth chuckled and settled comfortably.

Sidharth was busy playing a game on his phone when the instructor arrived and shook Shanaya stronger than he planned to. Shanaya sat up with her eyebrows furrowed, blinking. As her eyes adjusted to the light, she saw Sidharth's mischievous smile.

"What did you do?" Shanaya frowned at Sidharth, who was stopping himself from laughing.

"Nothing." He gave her a small smile.

"Sidharth Kapoor, I swear-"

"Nothing!! I was just laughing because of your just woken up face." Sidharth laughed softly and teased her more.

Sidharth moved his chair closer to Shanaya's and told her he leveled up in his game last night and he woke up in such a good mood even though he didn't get enough sleep. As much as Shanaya loved photography, she couldn't pay attention to it.

"Good for you. My morning was awful." Shanaya yawned and pouted.

"I know. I can see it in your face." Sidharth replied and continued talking about his game last night.

Shanaya was so hungry to listen to class that everything Sidharth said seemed more interesting, and it was just the second day so it's fine. She ranted to Sidharth about how her morning was and how she didn't have anything to eat. Sidharth listened to her and laughed seeing how frustrated Shanaya was.

Shanaya and Sidharth didn't even notice that the class had already ended until the surrounding people got up.

"I'll go to the cafeteria to grab something to eat. You want to go with me?" Shanaya asked as she gathered her things.

"Sure, my class doesn't start until an hour." Sidharth looked at the time on his watch.

"Let's go." Shanaya said and stood up as Sidharth grabbed his backpack. Shanaya smiled at Sidharth. Sidharth was a fresh sight to see, and his presence alone was something else. Shanaya badly missed being in the same school as Sidharth. Shanaya suddenly remembered all the memories she shared with Sidharth and giggled lightly.

"Hm?" Sidharth looked at her curiously.

"Nothing."

They walk along the corridors with people occasionally saying hi to Shanaya and snickering as they pass by.

"Why do you still even acknowledge them??" Sidharth asked, annoyed and looked at her.

"I don't, really. Most of them are in my class and the others are... I don't want to be rude." Shanaya replied nonchalantly. Sidharth said nothing at that, but rolled his eyes at Shanaya. His best friend was too good to be true.

They went down the stairs and turned right. Sidharth looked around the campus more and noticed that there were a lot of students compared to his old school. Some of them were familiar, but he really didn't know anyone that much.

"So, what time does your class end?" Sidharth looked at her.

"Around 5. You?"

"Hm quarter to 5. I'll wait for you at the garden bench?" Sidharth asked with a small smile.

Shanaya and Sidharth had met for the first time in Shanaya's senior year of high school. To say it was the most cliché combination would be an understatement. Shanaya was shy, the quiet nerd of the class. She always sat at the back of the class, nose buried in her journal and wore soft colored sweaters with sweater paws and wore glasses. Shanaya was afraid to get close to people because whenever they got close to her, it was always because they wanted some help or just to make fun of her. She didn't have any friends in the class and was a loner. Often after school, she would go in the park, look into the sky and cry to herself, thinking why was she like this. It was one of those days when a soft, warmhearted guy came and sat beside her and talked to her. That guy was Sidharth, and Sidharth was nothing like her. He was, in fact, the loud, extroverted popular guy every school has. The one everyone wants to talk to and get close to. Someone perfectly built even for such a young age and wore mostly black clothes. The one thing which was common to them was they both didn't do relationships.

Shanaya didn't do them simply because nobody ever asked and Sidharth had kindly always rejected them all. No one would have thought that one conversation in the dusk would bring these two people so close, but fate really did. They became best friends, even though Sidharth was two years younger than her. The age never really mattered to them. They would always talk for hours after school when they met at the park and it's been years since that incident, but some things never change and this was one of those things.

"Alright." Shanaya replied as they stepped into the cafeteria.

"What should I buy for today?" Sidharth placed a hand under his chin and looked around. Shanaya laughed at his silliness and noticed how the people that passed by them always looked at Sidharth. She cleared her throat. It was not like she never knew about it. Sidharth was handsome and was bound to become the next campus heartthrob that he finally transferred to her school. Shanaya already expected this much.

"I like their sandwich, it's good." Shanaya replied with a smile on her face as she wiggled her eyebrows.

Sidharth chuckled as Shanaya grabbed his hand and lined up with him to buy the sandwich. The line was long, but they both didn't mind, even if Shanaya's stomach was already grumbling.

"So why did you take up photography class? I thought you were going to art class this year." Shanaya asked as they took their places.

"There's no reason for it, really. You know I love taking photos and editing videos. Also, I already took art class last summer and eh." Sidharth replied, scrunching his nose.

"Fair enough." Shanaya chuckled, her eyes crinkling. She knew Sidharth would say that, but she never had the chance to ask him about it before. Sidharth didn't even tell her he was taking the same class as her until he suddenly brought it up when they were playing over watch together.

"Yup and you know how I am with editing. It's like you're getting sucked in and you can't get out until you finish it." His eyes glimmered as he talked about it. Shanaya looked at him, captivated. As always, her best friend looked beautiful whenever he talked about what he liked to do. One reason, she couldn't let go of the crush she had on him, even if she wanted to.

"I get you. I was like that last night watching anime." She replied jokingly.

"What did you watch last night? Is that why you didn't play with me?!?" Sidharth asked in disbelief and accidentally brushed Shanaya's hand softly on the table. They were sitting across from one another, and the table was tiny for their model figures.

"Well, that just happened." Shanaya smirked.

"How could you?" Sidharth narrowed his eyes at her and took a huge bite of his sandwich.

"This is superb, though." He added with his mouth full. Shanaya chuckled at him, endeared.

"I'll play with you after class. I promise."

"As you should." Sidharth said with a serious face.

"Yeah yeah."

Shanaya was always a little soft for Sidharth — Shanaya was always a little in love with him.

Sidharth had come to her life as a ray of sunshine. He comforted her at her worst and made her happy without even trying. Shanaya hadn't known what a real genuine friendship meant before she had met Sidharth. She had never thought that someone like him would ever even want to be friends with her, but now they were closer than ever. She truly cherished every moment she spent with him.

She wouldn't say it was love at first sight, but it was a feeling she knew nobody made her feel except Sidharth. Shanaya never confessed or even tried to portray her emotions to him because she was too scared to lose him. Maybe it was a bit selfish, but Sidharth had always been a source of love for her. Whether it was to love herself or the other. The first year in university was a little difficult for Shanaya because she didn't have anyone and she missed Sidharth, but after he joined the university too, she was naturally happy.

She still remembers that one time when she told Sidharth, it scared her to go to a university because she didn't know how the people would be and mostly because she won't have her best friend with her. Sidharth wasn't there to protect her or anything. She was capable enough for that herself, but his presence made a big difference to Shanaya. To that, the younger replied with "No worries Shanaya, I'll work really hard just to be in the same university as you and then you don't have to think about anything."

Shanaya laughed at it and passed it as a joke before, but Sidharth did really work hard just to be with her, even though he had dreamt of being at a different university from the beginning. These are the times she thinks to herself to be a little selfish about her feelings and tell them to Siddharth. Maybe they can be something more than friends? But again, these are also the moments where she falls for Sidharth even more than she is and she can't make herself to speak something which may make her to lose Sidharth. She may never be honest about it, but as long as she has Sidharth, she's just happy with it.

Shanaya yawned and continued scribbling on her notebook as she copied some information from several books that she needed for her homework. She had 2 hours vacant and worked on her assignment that was due tomorrow in the library. Even if it made her want to sleep, she loved the peace in the library. She yawned once more and was softly drifting off to sleep when there was a light tap on her table that made her snap her head up and look at who it was.

"You should finish your homework first." Sidharth smirked at her and took a seat on the chair across from Shanaya.

"I am. What are you talking about?" Shanaya sat up straight and cocked an eyebrow at him.

Sidharth chuckled, "I'll accompany you. My class is still in an hour."

"Sure." She smiled at him and continued her work.

Sidharth organized Shanaya's scattered things on the table, careful that he might disrupt the older in which Shanaya faintly coos at. Sidharth was always considerate and kind that it was so hard for her heart not to beat fast at those little actions he did for her. He was definitely the ultimate man that everyone wanted.

Sidharth was quietly working all throughout and occasionally glanced at Shanaya to see what she's doing that made her conscious most of the time. Shanaya pretended she didn't notice and continued with what she was doing as the younger gathered his things and placed them on the side and he rested his head on top of his arms on the table. Shanaya smiled softly and giggled at the sight.

"What?" Sidharth looked at her, pouting.

"You just told me a while ago to finish what I was doing before sleeping and now look at you." She chuckled and found the pout adorable, too.

"I will continue later. Hehe wakes me up soon." Sidharth settled comfortably and closed his eyes. Shanaya shook her head with a fond smile plastered on her face and continued working.

Shanaya looked at the time on her phone and stretched her arms. She looked at Sidharth, sleeping soundly across her. He was so beautiful and warm that she thought she could just stare at him the whole day and not tire of it. Shanaya rested her chin on her hand and looked at him, sleeping like a baby. How could someone still be so perfect even if they were asleep? Shanaya smiled adoringly as her eyes traveled to Sidharth's cheek. That was so hard to resist from squishing, to his perfectly sculpted nose, and to his pink lips that anyone would be lucky to have a taste. Shanaya felt her cheeks burn, and she sat up. She shook her head away from those ill thoughts and gathered her belongings. After a short while, she woke Sidharth up who had messy hair but was still ever so adorable.

Sidharth had always been beautiful to Shanaya. There was always something about him which made him more attractive than anyone had ever seemed to Shanaya. At first, she thought it was just a mere admiration for the younger, but as time passed, the admiration seemed to grow deeper and soon she realized it was something much deeper than that. She was much more into that. She was much more than just having a crush on Sidharth.

Sidharth was beautiful to her even when he was dirty from all the paint stains which Shanaya had put into him while Sidharth admired her work while she painted on him. And he was more beautiful in the night when he would sneak out of his home just to spend time with her. Sidharth was beautiful even when he was sad and when he was happy. He was beautiful, too.

One may call Shanaya smitten, but if she were to choose between who she found more beautiful between the god of beauty and Sidharth, Sidharth would still be more beautiful to her.

It wasn't just his face when he pouted or the way his eyes crinkled when he smiled. He was even beautiful when he cried over Shanaya's goldfish and when he got a first prize for his photography.

Sidharth was beautiful in a mess and he made a mess look beautiful. Shanaya, as the older one, always found it as her responsibility to take care of Sidharth ever since they were younger. She just didn't realize when this responsibility became so addicting that she didn't want to lose it. She didn't realize when Sidharth started meaning much more than he should have. There was no turning back when she fell in love with Sidharth.

$\heartsuit$

Shanaya told Kiya that Sidharth was in her photography class. Kiya was probably Shanaya's closest friend after Sidharth. Kiya knew about the tiny crush she had for Sidharth and how long it had been. Shanaya looked up at the blue sky as they were walking in the school garden after having lunch together. She was vacant for 2 more hours and Kiya had a class after an hour. She didn't get to see Sidharth for today yet, but she always does, every single day.

"So, your partner is back?" Kiya said, a teasing tone in her voice.

"Photography class partner, you mean? I was worried that I didn't have any friends in that class, but then Sidharth came along." Shanaya replied, smiling adoringly.

"Sounds like it's going to turn into a heart trouble, Shanu. You know how it was back in our old school. You always got jealous of people close to Sidharth that weren't you, well, except for me." Kiya raised an eyebrow at her.

"It's not Kiya." She rolled her eyes.

Kiya smirked at her. "I bet it will."

"Whatever, it really won't." Shanaya marched forward, leaving her behind.

"Wait up!!"

Shanaya checked the time on her watch. "I'll be at the library for the rest of the time before my class. You?"

"I'm going at the cafe near school. To plan a project, I have to meet up with some friends. I'll text you if I could hang out later." Kiya said in a rush as she turned to leave.

"Okay. See you."

Shanaya walked her way to the library, looking down at her steps. She always avoids making eye contact with people for fear that they might judge her. She was trying to take her phone from her bag when she bumped into a guy with a tall physique but has a stronger build which caused her to falter a bit.

The guy held her arm to steady her. She looked up and saw two doe eyes staring at her with concern, "Oh Shanaya, it's you."

"Sid!!" Shanaya exclaimed, balancing herself as Sidharth helped her.

"Sorry for that. I didn't notice you." Sidharth scratched the back of his head apologetically.

"No, no, I wasn't looking at where I was going. It's okay." Shanaya smiled at him. He was such a gentleman and just everything about him was almost perfect that she can't help but be in love with him.

"Where are you headed?" Sidharth began walking again with Shanaya beside him.

"Library. My class is still in about 40 minutes." Shanaya answered.

"Oh, I'm going there too!! Let's share a table." Sidharth smiled widely at her.

Shanaya laughed lightly at the younger's enthusiasm. He had always been really a great company and with Sidharth beside her; she dared to face forward and look at her surroundings. Sidharth was a sunshine to her, and she always felt better with him. Maybe she had a little crush ever since they were younger, but it was just an admiration, since Sidharth was amazing. Or so what she's been convincing herself when she knew at the back of her mind, Sidharth wasn't just that.

Shanaya had been hanging out with Sidharth the past few weeks and they always planned their meetings as if they had the same classes. They mostly hung out after all of it and did everything that they could think of. Sidharth would sometimes spend his vacant time at Shanaya's dorm, and she would also visit Sidharth's house.

"Sidharth!! Over here." Shanaya waved at Sidharth, who's looking around for her. She smiled widely at the sight of the younger.

Shanaya was in the campus garden with Kiya. She texted Sidharth to meet with her before their class together.

Sidharth waved back at her and headed over to where Shanaya and Kiya were.

"Hi Kiya Di." Sidharth said, smiling softly.

"Hey Sid." Kiya smiled back at him.

Shanaya laughed lightly at how formal the two were, even when they also shared a class. Kiya and Sidharth became friends because of her back then, and the three of them spent most of the time together. It was weird to see them uncomfortable with one another, but she knew that after giving it a few more minutes, it will be back to how it was before.

"Yeah, di. You got so busy with your dance class that you've forgotten all about me and Shanu." Sidharth jokingly said.

"I did not!! Tell him Shanu." Kiya replied defensively and poked Shanaya at the side.

"Hey!! Stop poking me. And it's true, you've been busy back then, which is why we spent more time together and are closer than you." Shanaya joined in the teasing and smiled mischievously.

"Therefore, I hate having the two of you together. You just gang up on me." Kiya glared at them and broke into laughter.

Sidharth laughed loudly and Shanaya joined in, too. The school bell rang, and they stood up, heading back to the campus.

"So, you actually got into this school because of Shanaya??" Kiya laughed, "It really surprised me when Shani told me you were here."

"I got into this school because I got accepted," Sidharth smirked, "and Shanaya, too. I missed you two and school was much more fun with both of you."

Shanaya never thought that she was partly the reason Sidharth transferred to her school, even when she thought about it. Her eyes crinkled at the corners, "I missed the three of us together too."

"And you are now more talkative now than when you're only with me. You talk a lot when you get really comfortable around people Shanaya, it's nice to hear." Kiya commented and patted her back.

"Mhm, I enjoy listening to you talk about random stuff all the time." Sidharth added, beaming at her.

Shanaya blushed a bit at the compliments, flattered at what they, said and eased her insecurity. She never knew they liked that quality of her she rarely shows to others and it was even more embarrassing that Sidharth did too. Sidharth was a hard man not to like when almost everything he does and says were endearing to her and just full of sincerity.

"You both have class together now, right?" Shanaya asked, looking at Kiya and Sidharth. They were on their way to their classrooms together.

"Yup." Kiya replied, unwrapping a candy.

"Why? You'll miss me?" Sidharth asked in a teasing manner.

"Of course not, idiot." Shanaya replied, sticking her tongue out at Sidharth.

"Aww it's okay to say your true feelings, Shanie." Sidharth teased, placing an arm around Shanaya's shoulder. The feeling was so familiar. She missed Sidharth, constantly goofing off around her. She smiled softly and nudged Sidharth off her as Kiya laughed out loud at the two.

"Hey stop bickering, you idiots!! Let's go Sidharth." Kiya said, still laughing as she tried to stop them.

"See you later Shanaya!! Meet me at the ghaat, love you!" Sidharth jokingly said and winked at Shanaya.

"Yeah, I hate you too, bye Kiyaaa!!" Shanaya smiled at the both of them.

She could feel her heart beating faster for Sidharth, but ignored the sensation. She has felt that in weeks, and just hearing his name would make Shanaya smile like an idiot. It was weird how Sidharth was always on her mind; she would unconsciously smile every time she thought of him and always wanted to talk to him and spend time with him. She would step out of her normal routine and make some extra time just to spend it with Sidharth.

Shanaya valued Sidharth's thoughts and opinions, maybe a little too much. If she got a new hairstyle or is wearing a new shirt, she always wants to know what Sidharth thinks. It's important to her. Shanaya always remembered everything Sidharth would say. It doesn't matter if it's totally irrelevant or super important. It felt like a priority to know as much as she can about Sidharth, and part of that is remembering the small things. And even though all of it may have meant that she really had loved Sidharth, she preferred to ignore it. It was just a small crush, that's it.

Shanaya saw Sidharth after her class at the school garden and saw that the younger had company. She was gonna go up to him and maybe ask if his class was over so they could go together, but decided not to when she saw the aura the two people in front of her gave off. They looked perfect for each other and she can't even deny the chemistry that they had. She slowly backed away and went ahead to their meeting place with a sad face.

Shanaya waited for Sidharth in the small take away stall by the Ganga Ghat. It was a small shop owned by an eighty-year- old grandma. It had always been there, even before they met. During their break time, they would go there to have Shanaya's favorite, momos. Then, it became a place for hanging out, which comprised only the two of them, and Shanaya thought they were always a bit more than friendly and just made her crush for the younger to grow even more.

"Siddd! I'm hungry!" Shanaya cried as Sidharth ran towards her.

"Come on, let's get your favorite momo." Sidharth said, grabbing her hand.

"What would I do without you, Sid?" She smiled at her friend. "Let's go."

At that moment, Shanaya was sure that it wasn't just a stupid little crush, but she was in fact in love with him. Because at that point, just being with him didn't feel enough. She really wanted to touch his skin and hug him and feel his warmth and smell his scent and feel how soft his hair was, to look into his eyes and hear his voice and just soak in his presence. Even though she knew it was impossible for Sidharth to like her back, she just wanted Sidharth to be hers' and be there for her and not just as her best friend, but maybe just a little more than that. But she knew she was asking for too much and she had to be content with just being how they were.

"Shani, you know I have a friend in my science class who told me she actually hated me for the first time, it's amazing, don't you think?" Sidharth said as he dipped his momo in the chutney.

"Hated you? Why?" Shanaya asked, looking at him with curiosity.

"I don't know, but it's kinda funny because we're great friends now." He said, a smile appearing at the corner of his mouth.

"She even told me that maybe she didn't hate me but was just intimidated when, in reality, I was the one who got intimidated by her." He chuckled.

Shanaya just listened to Sidharth talk about whoever that girl was. It was a whole new other side of Sidharth that she saw. He seemed much softer, like he was talking about someone that's close to his heart, as if being with that someone really made him happy and he wouldn't miss a chance to be with them. He was smiling in a way which seemed to be reserved only for that person, and he was talking in the same way about that girl as Shanaya talks about Sidharth to Kiya.

Shanaya remembered seeing Sidharth with a girl which she assumed was the girl Sidharth was talking about since he smiled so wide at him that his bunny smile was showing. She softly smiled at the sight of Sidharth genuinely being happy, but she couldn't help feeling sad, too. She wanted Sidharth to look at her that way, but it never was the case.

"Shanaya, you're living in a flat alone, right?" Sidharth asked as he munched on the noodle, bringing Shanaya out of her thoughts.

"Huh? Ah yeah, I might probably have to look for a flat-mate for the flat right next to me as my landlord requested me to find someone for it." Shanaya replied, her voice neutral. As much as she tried to think about being happy for Sidharth, it did still sting.

"Oh, that's a good thing. Do you want me to rent that out?" He asked with a mischievous smile.

"What?" She was bringing the momo to her mouth when she stopped midway because of what Siddharth just said.

"It's because you know I'm living with Nikhil Bhaiya right now and I think he's gonna be living with Shalini Di," Sidharth said. "I need to give them privacy, so I thought maybe I should stay in a dorm."

"But with me?!?? As in right next to me?"

"Why not? We'll have fun every day!!" He said happily and continued eating.

"You just want someone to wake you up in the morning." Shanaya shook her head. She's also convinced herself that this is just a plan yet and won't actually happen.

"Well, you're not wrong about that." Sidharth chuckled.

"Let me think about it." She replied, looking at him.

"Alright, I have to tell my brother about it, too. See you tomorrow!!" Sidharth waves at her and leaves after finishing his momo in a hurry.

Shanaya thought how cruel it was that she had to fall for someone she could never have a chance with. Sidharth was kind, fun to be with, scored great in every class, was good at sports, at drawing, in singing, in boxing, in photography, literally one could name anything and Sidharth was probably great at it; in Shanaya's eyes, Sidharth was perfect. Even though he was still a freshman, everyone seemed to love him, but those were not the reasons she loved him. Of course, some of those were reasons which made her appreciate him more, but why she really fell in love with him was because he was different. He didn't talk to Shanaya because she was good at studies and topped every class and made the best notes, rather these things never really mattered to him. He stayed with her even though no one at the university or even back then, thought Shanaya was cool to be with or that she was boring. In a world where Shanaya often felt that no one really loved her, maybe except Kiya, Sidharth was someone who made her forget that feeling most of the time. He genuinely cared for her and hung out with her and never cared about his reputation. He stayed with her because he liked her company and not because he could benefit from her. Shanaya sometimes felt guilty for having feelings for him because she knew Sidharth had no feelings for her. Sidharth thought of Shanaya as his best friend. To be fair, he treated Shanaya better than any best friend would ever treat another.

She loved being with Sidharth. His constant support gave Shanaya the strength to move on in her life, even though many things seemed to stop her and made her doubt herself. She just needed to be around him because without him it felt so empty, even though she hadn't even known him for that long. Shanaya loves to see him smile. What she loves even more is when she is the reason for it. She is ready to do any silly thing just to make Sidharth smile like that meant something; that she meant something to him.

Never had she expected Sidharth and her to get this close, but she can only feel blessed they did and now that Sidharth was asking her if he could stay right next to her, she didn't know what to do about it. How was she going to live in the same house with the one she was in love with and not be obvious about it? How is she gonna hide her feelings for Sidharth?

♡

Sidharth thought about the whole moving out of the house and living in a dorm thing. He really wanted to be independent and be closer to the university, so whenever he gets up late, he would arrive in no time. He dug deep into his pocket, looking for their house key instead of ringing the doorbell, knowing that his older brother might be in the middle of something serious, and opened the door.

He stepped in, took off his shoes, and heard a loud crash in the living room. Sidharth shook his head and sighed. His brother was a disaster. He walked to the living room and sat beside his brother.

"Bhaiya, I want to live in a dorm and be independent." Sidharth said suddenly and looked at Nikhil on the couch beside him, who was seriously watching the movie that's on the television.

"Huh? Suddenly?" Nikhil asked, looking at him questioningly.

"Yup and I've decided to be Shanaya's flat-mate." Sidharth grinned, looking at his brother.

"Shanaya? I thought you were going to be independent. Shanu will just end up taking care of you." Nikhil nagged at him, shaking his head.

"I am!! Besides, Shanu won't and Shalini di will move in next week, right? I should give you both privacy." Sidharth smirked at him.

"What? Sidharth, if that's the reason you're moving out, I won't allow you." Nikhil said sternly, with a light blush on his cheeks.

"Ah bhaiya!! It's not!! I just want to live closer to the school and I really want to live on my own. I'm in college already." Sidharth replied sincerely.

"Hmm, doubtful but alright, I'll call mom later to ask her but you have to officially ask her for permission, okay?" Nikhil sighed, ruffling Sidharth's hair.

"Yes!! Thank you bhaiya!!" Sidharth said cheerfully and jumped up from the couch. He showed his bunny smile, grabbed his backpack, and ran upstairs to his room.

Sidharth sprawled on his bed, texting Shanaya, "bhaiya says yes!! Have to ask mom though but I'm sure she'll say yes when I mention your name haha and she'll be happy with it."

But Sidharth doesn't get a reply and sees the message unread. He just thinks that maybe Shanaya is already fast asleep. He played over watch for a short while until he got sleepy and drifted to dreamland.

♡

Shanaya woke up late for her class and she only had merely 15 minutes to spare until it started. Good thing she was living in the university dorm that she only had to run really fast to get there on time. She caught her breath as she grabbed the doorknob and saw Sidharth running towards her.

"Oh? You're late too?" Sidharth said, panting, a smile on his lips.

"Yeah." Shanaya replied, turned the knob and entered the classroom. She only glanced at Sidharth and avoided eye contact. She received his text message yesterday but didn't know what to respond to yet. Should she tell him no? because what the hell? Or yes, because why the hell not?

As the class started and everyone settled down, Sidharth tried to get Shanaya's attention, who was focused on listening to the instructor and taking down notes.

"Shanu," Sidharth whispered, "Shanu!!" he whispered louder this time.

Shanaya furrowed her eyebrows and looked at him, mouthing a "what?"

Sidharth was about to say something when their instructor said they will have a 10 minutes break and resume right after.

Hearing that, Sidharth stood up to get closer to Shanaya.

"You haven't read my text?" He asked, bringing his desk closer to Shanaya's.

"You texted? About?" Shanaya pretended she didn't know about the message and avoided Sidharth's gaze. She could feel butterflies in her stomach as Sidharth got even closer that their elbows were almost touching.

"At least read my texts to you idiot." Sidharth nudged at her and chuckled, "Nikhil bhaiya agreed and I asked my mom for permission, and she also said yes!!" He said enthusiastically and his eyes sparkled with excitement.

"Oh, that's a good thing, then." Shanaya replied coolly but was actually internally breaking down. She planned to avoid this conversation the whole day but, well, what is Sidharth without persistence?

"So? Roomies?" Sidharth asked, smiling widely.

"I-"

Shanaya got cut off when the instructor started discussing again, saying that the break was over. She whispered "later" to Sidharth and listened to the discussion.

"We're now flat-mates, right?" Sidharth immediately asked Shanaya when the class got dismissed.

Shanaya just stared at him for a while, conflicted with what to answer. If she was gonna say yes, she had to deal with living in a small space with her best friend who became the one she loved more than just that, and maybe there's nothing wrong with that but she's worried that she might mess it up and slip that she has feelings for him. But if she was gonna say no, hell, how could she say no to the one she loves?

"Fine, let me clean up for a bit, then you can move in by Friday." Shanaya sighed and stood up. She can't actually say no to Sidharth just because of her stupid feelings, either.

"Alright!! Help me pack, okay? Thank you, Shani!!" Sidharth replied, hugging Shanaya.

Shanaya got surprised at the gesture and could feel her cheeks burning. She couldn't say anything.

Sidharth pulled away, and looked at Shanaya, who had flushed cheeks but didn't comment on it. "Let's go?"

Shanaya looked at the calendar and saw that it was finally Friday, the day that Sidharth would move into her dorm. Luckily, both of their classes for the day got canceled because of some school meeting. Shanaya planned to meet Sidharth at his house to get his belongings and help him with the rest of the packing.

When she accepted the younger's offer, she cleaned every corner of the dorm to make it more comfortable. She even bought light soap scented essential oils for the diffuser, knowing that Sidharth is sensitive to smell. She bought new clean sheets for him and other necessities that he might need in the dorm. When Shanaya finally finished arranging everything, she texted Sidharth that she's on the way to his house and got out of her dorm. Shanaya was excited, but she was also nervous, knowing that they'll be staying together in one place every day.

She was looking out the window on the bus when she received a reply from Sidharth, "okay! See you :D"

Shanaya smiled at the text message. It was such a Sidharth thing and decided not to reply. She was minutes away from seeing him, anyway.

Sidharth looked around at his stuff in his room with his hand under his chin, thinking of what else he should bring.

Nikhil opened the door to his room and saw his younger brother deep in thought, "Sid, you know you could just come back for your other things."

"But what if I need it when I get there?" Sidharth said, his eyebrows furrowed.

Suddenly, the doorbell rang, announcing that someone was at the door.

"I'll get it. It's probably Shanaya." Nikhil said and left Sidharth's room with the door open.

Shanaya placed her hands in her pockets and waited for someone to open the door. She stared at the small flower that bloomed, sticking out of the ground, and smiled softly until the door opened.

"Hey Shani, Sidharth's upstairs in his room." Nikhil said with a warm smile.

"He's not done yet?" Shanaya chuckled. Nikhil just gave her a shrug.

Shanaya visited Sidharth's house a lot of times way back when they were younger until now that they were older that Nikhil became her friend too. She also knew Shalini, who is Nikhil's girlfriend. She also used to sleep over at their house all the time when they've played games or were watching a movie too late.

"Hey, you need help?" Shanaya entered his room and saw Sidharth crouching, packing some of his things in his bag.

'So cute.' Shanaya thought and smiled softly.

"Just those last few things, then I'm done. What else do you think I need?" Sidharth looked up at her.

"I think you already have everything?" Shanaya chuckled and helped him with his last few stuff to pack.

"Okay, that's the last one." He stood up and stretched his arms. Shanaya smiled fondly at the sight and carried the other things for him as they got down the stairs.

"You're done? Finally?" Nikhil chuckled and helped them.

"Yup!!!" Sidharth replied with a huge smile on his face.

"Took quite a while, and he's bringing too much stuff that he probably won't need, but finally." Shanaya laughed.

"Sha, call me if you don't want him anymore, okay?" Nikhil said jokingly, patting her back.

"Of course bhaiya, I can also just kick him out of the dorm." She smirked and looked at Sidharth.

"Hey!! I'm literally right here???" Sidharth glared at the both of them as they laughed loudly.

"But seriously, take care alright? Call me if you need anything." Nikhil said, hugging his younger brother.

"Yes bhaiya, I'll come visit with Shanaya sometimes." Sidharth hugged him back.

"Take care of him for me, Sha, and thanks." Nikhil gave Shanaya a hug as well. He felt giddy as Nikhil said that it felt like he was giving their blessing as a couple. She shook her head, clearing herself from those thoughts.

They said their goodbyes and headed to the bus stop. Sidharth excitedly talked about how thrilled he was to be living in a dorm with his best friend and that he could do anything that he wanted. But Shanaya couldn't pay attention to what Sidharth was saying. Her heartbeat ringing in her ears was louder and her thoughts were overpowering it, too. She just occasionally nodded and laughed at what Sidharth said, even though she didn't understand any of it.

They finally arrived at Shanaya's dorm after struggling with carrying all the stuff Sidharth brought. Sidharth looked at her apologetically and Shanaya just giggled at him.

"You've already been here a couple of times so I think you already know what it looks like." Shanaya opened the door as she felt anxious that Sidharth might not like it and change his mind.

"Woah, you really cleaned up the place!! And it smells so good. I love it." Sidharth looked around the place, smiling.

"I've also cleaned your bed, so it's ready to use." Shanaya said shyly.

"The bedsheets smell good too and it's so clean!! Thank you Shanu!!" Sidharth said as he plopped on his bed, his bunny smile showing.

Shanaya could feel her heart going wild seeing that smile again. Sidharth looked beautiful and adorable whenever he smiled like that. Shanaya thought she was really lucky to have him and to like him.

"Let's order some pizza and ice cream? To celebrate your first day here?" She said with a fond smile, a soft blush on her cheeks.

"Yes!! I'd have cookies and cream," Sidharth replied, and sat up. "You're the best Sha. Thank you." A warm smile playing at the corners of his mouth.

Shanaya looked away, blushing even more. She said a soft "you're welcome" and made a call for delivery.

Sidharth unpacked his belongings and Shanaya was setting up the movie when a knock on the door resounded, Shanaya and Sidharth stared at each other and bursted into an enormous laughter right after. Shanaya stood up to receive the food delivery and placed it on the table in their mini living room.

"We should've bought some beer." Sidharth vibrantly took the ice cream out of the plastic bag and handed Shanaya a spoon.

"We have class tomorrow." Shanaya hummed softly.

Sidharth was ready to scoop the ice cream from its container when Shanaya stopped him. "Wait!!!! Don't move."

"Huh??"

Shanaya giggled at the surprised look on Sidharth's face and quickly grabbed her polaroid instant camera, "smile for the camera first. This is the perfect welcoming photo moment."

"Heh of course." Sidharth grinned.

Shanaya always took a picture of their moments together ever since Sidharth gave her that camera as a gift when she graduated from high school. It was when her eyes sparkled and She looked at the younger with fondness and love. She turned the camera so that the lens faced them and they scooted closer together to be included in the frame.

"Okay 1! 2! 3! Welcome Sid!!"

The camera shutter flashed, and the film came out slowly, the image still in a blur.

"Can I dig in now?" Sidharth pleaded, looking at Shanaya with puppy eyes.

Shanaya cracked a laughter and settled beside Sidharth, opening the pizza box. The polaroid was at the side, revealing two genuine smiling faces with one throwing up a peace sign.

"Sha!! Wake up!! You're gonna be late!!" Sidharth shook Shanaya, trying to wake her up as he buttoned up his shirt.

"What?" Shanaya asked, her eyebrows furrowed in confusion.

"Wake up!! Come on." Sidharth grabbed her hand, helping her sit up.

It had almost been a month since they lived together. Shanaya is usually the one that wakes Sidharth up, but for the first time, it was the other way around.

"Shit!!" Shanaya glanced at her bedside clock and sprang up. She only had 15 minutes to spare. She quickly changed into a new clean shirt and slipped into her jeans. And didn't care if she didn't get to take a shower. She couldn't afford to be late for this class that she had an exam in.

"Good morning to you." Sidharth smirked, looking at Shanaya going back and forth as he munched on a toast.

"You won't go yet?" She asked him, grabbing a piece of bread.

"Nope, my first class got canceled, and I forgot about it. Kind of good thing, though, I've woken you up." Sidharth grins.

"Thank you, I owe you." Shanaya melted at the gesture, "see you later!!" she shouted as she got out of the dorm.

Shanaya looked around the campus in search of Sidharth, who wasn't responding to her text messages when she bumped into Kiya. She just finished her class and was planning to go with the younger somewhere but didn't get any reply.

"Have you seen Sidharth?" Shanaya asked Kiya who was walking beside her.

"Sidharth? I had a class with him a while ago and he was with Yoona? That girl from his science class?" Kiya replied.

"Hmm, okay," Shanaya said, looking around, trying to find Sidharth.

Shanaya eventually sees the figure of Sidharth. She raised her hand, ready to call out to him when she saw a girl beside him, smaller in height, looked soft, and delicate than she was.

"I owe you a lot." Yoona said to Sidharth as she tightened her hold around the books that she's carrying.

Sidharth laughed heartily, "It's fine, Yoona, I would always be glad to help you."

"But really, I will make it up to you soon." Yoona blushed lightly and shyly looked away.

"Okay, if it makes you feel better." Sidharth brushed his hand through his hair with a small, fond smile on his lips.

"I um I guess I better get going?" Yoona said, the blush still visible on her cheeks.

"Oh right! Of course, I'll see you around!" Sidharth waved goodbye, his bunny smile plastered on his face.

Shanaya saw the entire scenario, the way Sidharth was laughing warmly at what the girl said, the slight blush on the girls's cheek as Sidharth said something to her and when she bid a goodbye. Shanaya looked away at that. She could feel her heart crush, and continued walking with Kiya by her side.

Sidharth spotted Shanaya from afar and hurried to catch up to her. And also saw Kiya beside her. He was having a really great day, plus that encounter with his little admiration for Yoona.

"What should we do today?" Sidharth suddenly appeared, placing an arm around Shanaya's shoulder.

"Hey, I was just looking for you," Shanaya said with a subtle smile.

"Oh, I was with Yoona, the one I told you about? She thanked me for something and told me about this new cafe that opened up and she wanted me to go with her since she thinks she owes me when it's actually really fine." Sidharth flashed a wide smile.

Shanaya's smile slowly turned into a frown. She swallowed hard. Sidharth had been talking about that girl all the time and she can't help but feel that this girl was taking Sidharth away from her. It made her feel a little jealous to see someone getting a sort of reaction she had always wished for herself. But Shanaya also knew that if it's someone Sidharth likes, then she must be really special and probably a lot better than her, even if she wished the person was her. She was just happy because at least one of them was happy and could be with the one they love. And Shanaya was happy it was him.

"Let's play games today?" Sidharth looked at her, his eyes soft and oblivious to Shanaya's reaction.

"S-sure." Shanaya stammered and looked away.

Kiya looked at Shanaya, then at Sidharth and realised something, but said nothing about it. She whistled and shook her head.

"Um, I'll go this way. See you tomorrow." Kiya waved at them with a warm smile as she turned at a corner.

They go their separate ways with Sidharth's arm still draped around Shanaya's shoulder.

"Should we buy some drinks before we head home?" Sidharth asked, looking at Shanaya.

"Okay, let's buy some snacks too." Shanaya replied, slightly smiling. She still felt sad, but there was no use dwelling on it. She's happy if Sidharth's happy.

At least she had these moments with him. She could hear how Sidharth referred to them as 'we' and talk about 'their' home, which she loved the most. She already accepted the fact that they were only gonna be best friends and she didn't want to ruin anything between them.

Shanaya and Sidharth stopped by the nearest convenience store. They've been here a lot of times whenever they craved for a certain food, this store always had it. And they always go there together. They quickly buy what they need and race each other back to their dorm.

Sidharth looked at the show on the television boringly. He's been waiting for Shanaya to finish her business in the bathroom so they could start eating the food they bought and play some games.

"Let's play!!" Sidharth shouted as Shanaya got out of the bathroom.

"Okay, okay!!" she replied, sitting beside him on the couch as they played the game.

"Do go easy on me, my dude," Sidharth said, a smug expression on his face.

"Shut up. I should be the one telling you that."

"Uh oh."

"Hey!!! That's cheating!!" Shanaya said as Sidharth took her phone away.

They were still playing the mobile game, but Sidharth was losing. He took Shanaya's phone and raised it over his head, preventing her from taking it. Shanaya still reached over it and grabbed it, stumbling over Sidharth.

Shanaya noticed their position. Her eyes widened and cheeks flushed. Her foolish heart beating crazily again, as usual. Sidharth said an "ow" and laughed at that. He doesn't even mind the position with Shanaya on top of him. She lightly laughs with Sidharth, playfully hitting him and sat up, pretending like that didn't make her heart drop.

They eventually called it a night and turned off the lights as they snuggled with their pillows and plushes on the small couch in their own home.

Sidharth sat beside Shanaya during the class as usual. Sidharth was wearing a black polo t-shirt with light blue ripped jeans that day and kept messing with his hair during the class while he concentrated on his assignment.

Shanaya, who usually was the most attentive during the class, failed to pay attention that day as she kept staring at Sidharth. She was content with just looking at him like this. Being so close to him that everything else didn't matter. She didn't realise how long she kept staring for the younger to notice it and asked her what happened as he raised his eyebrows with his usual smirk.

That goddamn smirk always took Shanaya's breath away.

Shanaya didn't answer and looked away, pretending to concentrate on what the instructor said. Her unrequited crush was going to get her screwed someday. It was getting harder to cover up her feelings for him, especially when Sidharth was constantly by her side.

As their shared class ended, they got out of the room and walked together. Sidharth asked Shanaya out of the blue, "You wanna say something to me? Even during the class, you kept staring at me, so maybe you had something you wanted to say?"

"I love you," Shanaya whispered so softly that only she can hear it.

"What?" Sidharth asked, looking at her.

"I mean I love what you're wearing, I love your shoes too and you too. I mean you are really nice and the best friend I could ever ask for um... I'll leave first... I'm sorry," Shanaya stammered.

Shanaya walked away, but turned when Sidharth called her name from behind.

"You are really cute, Sha," Sidharth said with his cutest bunny smile.

"Thank you and you too. I mean that's really very sweet and cute of you to say that," Shanaya replied shyly trying to hide her blush as much as she could but clearly failed.

"Seriously, you're too cute. I have another class in ten, so I'll leave. Meet you at home, baby bear." Sidharth squished her cheeks softly before leaving a dumbfounded Shanaya on her feet with his hands on her cheeks.

Did Sidharth just squish her cheeks and call her cute? Did that mean he likes her too?

Shanaya slapped her cheeks and shook her head. It was impossible to happen, and she needs to stop daydreaming. Maybe Sidharth was just teasing her, yeah that was it. She smiled sadly and walked away.

When Shanaya entered her dorm later that night after studying in the library, she found Sidharth sitting by the desk, which usually stays empty. Shanaya felt giddy when she looked at him, who looked really beautiful in the dim light of the study table, concentrating on whatever he was writing. His specs had slightly lowered from the bridge of his nose and she was having an urge to bring it back to its place. She had never seen Sidharth wear glasses before. Usually, the younger looked pretty hot but today in glasses, he looked really cute to him.

She must have made her presence obvious by the sound she made while closing the door, because Sidharth turned to look at her.

"Oh, you're back? I was waiting for you to arrive. I'm super sleepy but I've left the food on the table so heat it before eating, okay? Sorry I ate without you," Sidharth said and left to settle on his bed, yawning.

Shanaya didn't know what happened to her, but she froze on the spot. For how long? She doesn't know. But it must have been long enough for Sidharth to turn off the lights and lie on his bed for a peaceful slumber.

Shanaya really needs to get a hold of herself, she thought as she settled on her own bed that night. She didn't sleep looking at the moon that night but slept, to Sidharth's thought, running in her head.

♡

Sidharth and Shanaya were sitting next to each other with their legs tangled on the couch. It was Saturday, and it had been a few weeks since, even though this was something friendly for Sidharth, it still made Shanaya feel butterflies. All this time she had tried her best to not be obvious, and she gave herself credit that she was doing a good job of not making Sidharth uncomfortable. In fact, as days passed, Sidharth seemed to get more comfortable with her in the small space they live in. It almost felt surreal how domestically they acted around each other. They would have meals together, play games, and help each other with their studies. But what Shanaya liked the most was their movie nights which eventually became nights, where they would keep talking until the early hours of the morning. For Sidharth, it always had been platonic, but each of these brief moments made Shanaya fall deeper for him every single day.

Shanaya was on her way to the cafe near their dorm to meet up with Hrithik, who was her classmate and partner for a project in Science. They were good friends, and she always found Hrithik to be bubbly and popular with everyone, like how Sidharth was. He was also the guy who always had a girlfriend, unlike Shanaya, who has been single for as long as she has existed.

"Sha!!" Hrithik waved at her with a wide smile on his face.

"Thanks for waiting," Shanaya gave him a slight smile, and placed her things. "You're only gonna have that?"

"Yup, I like this drink and I don't wanna eat. Go buy something for yourself."

Hrithik gave her a thumbs up and a proud smile. Shanaya just giggled slightly and nodded, heading to the counter.

"Oooh, I didn't know you liked coffee, Sha."

"It tastes good and keeps me awake."

"True. Shall we start?"

"Of course. Do you have any ideas for the project?" Shanaya asked as she took out her notebook and pen.

"Ah yes, how about we set up an experiment booth?" Hrithik places a hand under his chin, thinking seriously.

"I don't-" She was about to say something when Hrithik's phone went off and took the call, in front of her as he mouthed "it's gonna be quick" to her.

"I'm busy with a project. We can see each other tomorrow." Hrithik says to the person on the other line.

Shanaya didn't want to listen in, but she couldn't help it when she was so near and she could hear them talking clearly.

"I know you miss me and all that, but I'm just busy for today. I'll see you tomorrow. Love you too."

Shanaya lowered her head and quietly drank her coffee as Hrithik hung up his phone. She thought of asking him about his love life, knowing that he had a lot of experiences in the past.

"Sorry, it was my girlfriend." Hrithik chuckled.

"Um, can I ask you something?"

"What is it?"

"Have you ever experienced being in an unrequited love?" Shanaya asked as she looked at Hrithik with sparkling, curious eyes.

"Of course!! Who hasn't? Unrequited love hurts a lot." Hrithik smiled sadly at her.

"Then do you think giving up is the best option?"

"That entirely depends on who you're in love with. There are those people that you're in an unrequited love with, but they don't know your existence and all of it is just superficial that still hurts but doesn't hurt that much. And the unrequited love that hurts the most, which comes from the people closest to you, those that you're in too deep and you don't know if you'd want to risk it. Hm with your question, if it's just superficial, time will come where it will fade or you'll find someone else. If you're already in too deep, I don't know. It's hard to take the risk of losing someone you love. It's a rare chance that they end up feeling the same way, you know? Most of the time, they just see you as family, that one person important to them but never their lover. The decision is entirely upon you. If you'd want to take the risk, you should be ready about the consequences and if you just want to keep whatever you have, you should be ready to accept the pain that it will bring and let time heal you. At least you'll still have them, right?" Hrithik smiled brightly and took a sip of his lemonade.

Shanaya smiled back at him sadly, not saying anything, and lowered her eyes. Everything that Hrithik told her was right. It was a risk to tell, and giving up was the only option to keep Sidharth in her life. So, what, they were just best friends? At least she was someone to the one that she loves, even if her heart was entirely breaking and she always suffers in silence.

Shanaya could never handle alcohol, but today was one of those days where she wanted to get drunk and even though Sidharth knew about Shanaya's low alcohol tolerance, he couldn't refuse his best friend's request. Shanaya meant a lot to him and he knew how the older wasn't the most popular girl on campus and therefore he felt like it was his duty as her best friend to protect her. Even though he had made a lot of friends since he joined the campus, no one was as pure and innocent as Shanaya, and even though she pretended in front of Sidharth that she was fine, he knew that a lot of things bothered her. He just wished he could know what it was and be able to help somehow.

"Do you think anyone can ever fall in love with me?" Shanaya asked suddenly, staring at the can of beer in her hand.

"What type of question is that, Sha? Of course, anyone would be a fool to not fall in love with you. You're intelligent, you're kind, you're so beautiful. Have you even looked at that face of yours?! And your hands are the most beautiful hands in the world. Anyone would be lucky to hold it and proudly say that they belong to you. But my best friend has the most beautiful heart, and how can someone not fall for that, huh?"

"Then why can't you fall in love with me, too?" Shanaya had tears brimming in her eyes.

"Sha, I-I think you're too drunk and not in your right mind and you should sleep. I shouldn't have let you drink too much. I'll take you to your bed and go to sleep, okay?"

"See I know you just say all this because you d-don't want me to feel b-bad but even though you're my b-best friend, you can't fall in love with me, then h-how will someone else haha," Shanaya laughed silently through her tears and Sidharth carried her, taking her to her bed.

"You know everyone thinks that I'm supposed to be lonely because why would someone like a nerd like me, right? Why would they wanna s-stay with a boring person like me? But don't I wanna f-feel loved too, huh? Can't I-I have feelings too? It's so funny that I want it so much. Even I want to have someone who'll call me mine b-but I know that will never happen. I'll never be loved-" Shanaya passed out, leaving the sentence incomplete.

Sidharth didn't know what to feel about what Shanaya had just confessed in her drunk state. Did she feel unloved and no one would ever love her? And did she want Sidharth to fall in love with her? He didn't know how to let that information settle.

Sidharth loves Shanaya, but he doesn't see Shanaya the way she wanted him to. Hell, if he could just fall in love with someone with his own wish, he would have, because he hated seeing Shanaya broken like that. But who has ever had control of their feelings alone? Who has ever fallen in love and actually fell in love with that certain someone? Even though Shanaya was beautiful inside out, he could never see her in that light.

That night when he settled beside Shanaya and brushed his fingers through his hair, he could just hope that when morning comes, everything would be like how it was before Shanaya had confessed about her feelings. That whatever he assumed through Shanaya's confession was not Shanaya's genuine feelings and it was just a momentary thing, and that Shanaya didn't really feel unloved. And even if they were real, Shanaya shouldn't like Sidharth or expect him to fall in love with her. Because no matter how much he hated seeing his best friend hurt and especially because of him, he knew he just couldn't give Shanaya what she wished for him.

"Ugh, my head hurts." Shanaya slowly got up, pressing her temple. She's feeling the hangover from their drinking session yesterday and swore never to drink that much again.

Shanaya doesn't find Sidharth anywhere in their dorm but sees a note in his handwriting on the table, "I'm buying something at the convenience store, brb." By the time she read the note, the door opened and Sidharth entered the dorm.

"Oh, you're awake." Sidharth said, closing the door.

"Did you buy something hot? My head hurts so bad." Shanaya pouts at him.

"Uh yeah."

Sidharth placed the porridge that he bought for the two of them on the table and took the seat across from Shanaya.

"Ah, this makes it so much better." Shanaya brings a spoonful into her mouth.

Sidharth says nothing, but just observes. He doesn't know what to say after what he heard from Shanaya yesterday.

"We'll buy groceries today? It's Sunday," Shanaya asked, bringing Sidharth out of his thoughts.

"Ah yeah, after a while we could go," Sidharth replied.

"What's with you today? Are you sick?" Shanaya chuckled.

She gets up, takes the hangover medicine and heads to the bathroom. Sidharth stayed there, still lingering in his thoughts. He doesn't know if Shanaya forgot about what happened yesterday or if she's just pretending, but he decided that he'll try to go along with it.

"What should we buy? What do we need at home?" Shanaya asked Sidharth as they rode the bus on the way to the supermarket.

"We need eggs, ramen, meat, and shampoo, soap. What else?" Sidharth asked, listing everything that he could think of on his phone.

"Hmm, bread, toothpaste, tissue, and ice cream?" She looked at him with a big smile on her face. She always loved how domestic they were, even if months had already passed by.

'One of the few advantages of being roommates with your crush,' Shanaya thought.

"Okay, then we'll know what else we need when we see them." Sidharth said, smiling back at her.

"We need cereals," Sidharth says and looks at Shanaya. Shanaya goes the other way to look for cereals as she lines up at the counter.

"Here, I got it." Shanaya dropped the cereals on the cart and waited with Sidharth as their items got scanned.

After a short while, they finished with their grocery shopping and were planning to head back to their place when Shanaya stopped walking.

"Let's drop by a cake shop. I wanna buy a small piece," Shanaya gives him a slight smile.

They stopped by a small cake shop and Sidharth waited outside. Shanaya said that it's gonna be quick, so he didn't mind at all.

"Let's go?" Shanaya said as she got out of the store bringing a small box of cake.

"Who's it for?" Sidharth asked, his eyes full of curiosity.

"Someone," she hummed, smiling.

"Hm okay." Sidharth replied, shrugging it off, and they headed home.

While Sidharth was busy arranging the groceries, Shanaya had been placing the toiletries in the bathroom. Since Shanaya finished her work faster, she helped him and placed the cake on the table while Sidharth was still busy with the last bit of the groceries.

"Actually, this cake is for you." Shanaya said, breaking the silence and shyly looking at Sidharth.

"Me? Why?" Sidharth asked, raising his eyebrows. When he had seen the cake a while ago, he really hadn't expected it to be for him. All this while he thought it was for someone else and didn't bother Shanaya asking more about it.

"For taking care of me yesterday and every day," the older replied softly.

That's when Sidharth noticed how careful Shanaya is with him and how she takes good care of him in the most subtle way. But he brushed it off and thought that Shanaya is always like that with everyone.

"Thank you, Sha, we should share this though," Sidharth smiled at her with a softness in his eyes.

Shanaya could feel her stomach doing somersaults and a blush was slowly creeping up her cheeks. She looked down to avoid getting caught and said a sheepish, "okay."

"Yoona also gave me a cake like this one yesterday." Sidharth began talking as he took a slice.

"Oh really? The one in your science class?" Shanaya asked, studying Sidharth's face and expression. She noticed how Sidharth's smile reached his eyes and crinkled at the sides.

"Mhm, she wanted to thank me for helping her with our exam. I've been tutoring her the past few weeks." Sidharth spares a little smile. He remembers those moments and how his heart fluttered at those.

Shanaya said nothing and continued eating the cake. She looked away as she noticed the younger deep in his thoughts. It shouldn't hurt her that much when she already knew about it, but seeing how different Sidharth was, she could feel her heart shattering.

♡

"Sid!! You have a class next?" Shanaya jogs towards Sidharth and catches up to him.

They didn't have any shared class today, and Sidharth had a class earlier than she did, so this was their first meeting for the day. Shanaya just even found Sidharth in the hallway by pure coincidence since she didn't get to text him. Shanaya smiled at how destiny brought them together. It's kind of funny, but you always think of the smallest thing whenever it's about your crush.

"Yes Shanu, you?" Sidharth said, holding the strap of his backpack.

"Same, will probably end up even later than it should." Shanaya looked at him like he held the stars in his eyes. Sidharth never realised how she looked at him longer than necessary until now.

"This is my last class for the day. Do you want me to wait for you?" Sidharth asked, looking away.

"No, it's okay. I'll see you at home," Shanaya replied delicately, smiling fondly at him. Sidharth also noticed how Shanaya talks softer with him than others, how gentle she is for him.

"Oh Sidharth! Shanu!!" Kiya shouted as she ran towards them.

"Hey!! You didn't wait for me." She pouts, hitting Shanaya on her shoulder when she has caught up with them.

"Ow!! You were so late and I was looking for Sidharth." Shanaya rubbed her shoulder from where Kiya hit her.

"Poor Sid," Kiya says jokingly, looking at Sidharth, "she always talks about you too, like all the time!! I'm tired of it."

"All the time?" Sidharth chuckled.

Shanaya was speechless. Her face glowed red. She avoided the gaze of the two who looked at her for answers and got saved by the resounding bell.

The school bell rang once again, cutting off their conversation. Sidharth waved goodbye and walked to his class. It was then that he noticed how

Shanaya always smiled at him, the smile she had only for him. The smile that speaks volumes.

Sidharth wasn't that blind, but he just thought Shanaya was like that to everyone. He really put little meaning behind them before, but that might change now. Sidharth sighed and thought about how he didn't want to be awkward with the older that he forgot about what happened that drunken night. And there was no use bringing it up since it looked like Shanaya forgot about it, too. He pushed the thought away and went inside the classroom.

Shanaya headed to photography class alone. Sidharth arrived after a few minutes, taking a glance at him. She sat in her seat and noticed the enormous gap between the two of them until Shanaya moved closer.

Every time he was with Shanaya, everything seemed to flow naturally. And what he regrets the most is he doesn't feel the same way as she wants him to or expects him to.

Sidharth just loved having Shanaya's attention and giving it to him. Her attention and love and appreciation towards him could make his day in a snap. He just wants Shanaya to feel special because she is special and just her existence itself makes Sidharth what he is. She is that important person in his life and he just wants to be part of her life too, even though one may not see it that way, but that's what it is. Be it in a small way, but still there. In her life, in her heart. Just in her.

Sidharth just felt the need for Shanaya in his life. Her constant support gave him strength to move on in life, even though there may be a lot of things to stop him. He just felt the need for this one girl constantly in his life. One day without her and his life just seems so empty.

Shanaya is the only person whom he says "I love you" daily, and it still feels so less. He wants her to know how much he loves her and how much she means to him and how he can do anything for her. Sidharth didn't say those words just for the sake of saying it, but because he feels it.

She was like his soulmate. She makes him a better person. Inspires him, understands him. No one can ever make him feel the way Shanaya does.

When you meet someone, you never know what's your future is with them. But with Shanaya, Sidharth wants his future with her. And her opinion matters the most to him.

He was ready to change himself for her. He hates hurting Shanaya. Not because he loves her romantically or something, but because when he sees her hurt, it hurts him even more – much, more. Sidharth feels something which seems like someone just stabbed him. He feels the pain even though no one caused him that.

Shanaya's happiness is his number one priority. What matters to him is just the older's happiness. But what made him happy the most was when he was the reason for Shanaya's happiness. When Shanaya smiles because of him. He is ready to do any stupidity just to see Shanaya smile because seeing Shanaya happy makes him happy.

Sidharth doesn't think about her, but still she is always stuck in his mind. Just randomly out of nowhere, he thinks about Shanaya, feeling about her. He doesn't do it, but he can't resist to that either. It just naturally happens.

He always wants to talk to her. About everything. He just wants to be silly with her. But he wants to talk about Shanaya with everyone but her. Maybe it's a way to show or stupidly prove the point that he knows everything about the older. He loves everything about Shanaya. Every minor detail. Be it those beautiful eyes, those bread cheeks or those pink lips, or maybe just all of her?

And when all of it just happens, how can it ever be an act? How can Sidharth pretend any of it when he can feel his heart beating for Shanaya at every point? Can Shanaya not know how Sidharth really feels when all these feelings he ever feels are because of her? How can he call it an act when it was never an act in the first place?

Sidharth knew they were meant to be, but not romantically. The love they had for each other existed, but it wasn't meant to turn into something more than friendship. It wasn't meant to hurt either of them, but it soothed them.

Is it so hard for him to accept the love he could only give and not ask for more? Is it so hard to understand that this love can exist between two people without hurting the other?

"Have you all planned for your photography project? I'll give you free time today to plan for it," the instructor said, bringing Sidharth out of his deep thoughts.

Shanaya groaned. She just realised that her partner for this was Sidharth and even if that was convenient for her, she couldn't stay with him much longer in fear of drowning in her own feelings. She turned to look at the younger who was already looking at her.

"Any plans?" Sidharth asked, scooting over.

"We just need to take a picture of a thing we love, right? We could just choose something in our dorm." Shanaya replied as she took notes on her notepad. She does her best not to turn red like she always does in the presence of Sidharth.

"I think we have to find a scenery that we love and capture it."

Shanaya looked at him and softly asked, "well, what scenery do you want?"

"The ocean." Sidharth said and looked back at her.

"Hm, okay, we could go there by tomorrow after class. It'll just take us a few minutes to travel, anyway." Shanaya responded nonchalantly, but her heart was beating wildly at that. She loved the ocean, and even more so with Sidharth.

"Okay."

Sidharth's class finished first, so he waited for Shanaya at the school gardens. He was cleaning his camera lens when Shanaya showed up in front of him.

"Let's get this over with," Shanaya said, holding out her hand for Sidharth. She was feeling brave for once and acted on the spot.

Sidharth sighed, a slight smile on his face, and grabbed her hand.

The bus ride to the ocean was only about 40 minutes. Shanaya wanted to sit somewhere else and not beside Sidharth, but Sidharth sat on the seat beside her unconsciously.

"Why are you sitting here?" Shanaya's voice raised a bit. Why was she acting like this? It's not like this is something new to them?

"Ah, sorry, there's no other vacant chair."

Shanaya nodded and looked out of the window, her cheeks burning. She loves and hates how she loves Sidharth with her whole heart.

Shanaya was lost in her thoughts when she felt something heavy on her shoulder. She turned to see Sidharth sleeping soundly. Sidharth always looked like an angel when he's asleep and like a baby that's so adorable you can't resist. Shanaya raised her hand to lightly touch his cheek, but before she could, she stopped herself and flushed. She lingered and looked away.

"Hey, we've arrived." Shanaya shakes Sidharth softly.

"Hm?" Sidharth opened his eyes gently and sat up, blinking. He realised it was almost sunset, "I fell asleep?? Sorry."

"Get up, we have to go. It's almost nighttime."

Sidharth ran towards the beach with Shanaya following him from behind. He stopped in front of the ocean, opened his arms wide, closed his eyes, and felt the air embrace him. Shanaya looked at him and the horizon. The view was beautiful and even more with Sidharth in it. She took a picture of the scenery in front of her and went to the younger.

"It's so beautiful. I missed this view." Shanaya said, breathing in.

"Me too." Sidharth captured the view a lot of times and looked around to take more photos.

Shanaya took a deep breath. The view was relaxing and breathtaking. She watched as the water got in her shoes and smiled softly. The ocean eating up the sun was beautiful to look at. Sunsets symbolize the end of the day, and Shanaya thought that being here together with Sidharth was the ending of their friendship too and maybe a new beginning to something more.

Sidharth stopped in his tracks and stared at Shanaya's back. He never realised how beautiful she was under the sunset and how her hair shined because of it. Shanaya has been on his mind a lot lately and he just couldn't seem to get her out of it. He enjoyed looking at her beautiful face. He liked looking into Shanaya's eyes to not only look at the smile on her face, but to just admire her fine features. Just looking at her wavy hair makes him want to stick his fingers in it, but he doesn't want to mess it up just because of how pretty it is. He captured the moment in his camera and was gonna go to Shanaya to let her see, but stopped himself.

"Let's go?" Shanaya asked, smiling fondly at him.

"Okay." Sidharth replied with a warm smile.

Shanaya woke up before her alarm sounded and looked at Sidharth beside her on the couch. She remembers how they were both playing a game together the night before and Sidharth settling beside her on her bed because it was comfortable. There was heavy rain that night and Sidharth loved being close to the window whenever it happened, so he stayed by Shanaya's bed.

Shanaya propped her hand on his cheeks, staring at Sidharth sleeping soundly. She thinks she could get used to this kind of view every single day with Sidharth so close to her. She looked at him endearingly and slowly brought up her hand to brush the hair from Sidharth's face when the younger moved, scrunching his nose.

Shanaya backed away, startled. She pretended nothing happened when Sidharth grabbed her wrist. "Why are you up so early?" Sidharth said in a deep voice.

"I- uh I just woke up a while ago," Shanaya stuttered, and got up from the bed.

"I will take a bath first and head to class. I-I have class early today," she added.

Sidharth nodded, rubbing his eyes and stretching his arms. If he wasn't too out of it, he could have noticed how Shanaya's face grew redder and how she was so conscious around him.

Shanaya and Kiya have a shared class today. They meet each other at the campus garden like they always do. Shanaya was waiting for Kiya to arrive when she remembered what happened last night and early in the morning again. She slapped her cheeks with both of her hands, shaking her head, when Kiya arrived and caught her in the act.

"Sidharth trouble again?" Kiya said, a smirk playing on her lips. Kiya held her hand out for Shanaya to help her get up.

"I think I'm falling deeper, Kiya," Shanaya grabbed her hand and stood up. They walked towards the campus and sat on the benches by the entrance.

"Hm, why don't you just confess to him?"

Shanaya snapped her head at Kiya, and looked at her in horror, "you know I can't do that!!"

"Why not? I think he likes you and I've been with both of you since before. I see it but I don't think Sidharth realizes it yet." Kiya said, smiling.

"That's what you think. I think he likes someone else and besides that, I can never be with someone like him. I can only dream." Shanaya heaved a deep sigh.

"Good thing that you know," a guy who had always bullied Shanaya for every little thing interrupted their conversation, "Sidharth is too good for someone like you."

"How can you even think he likes you? He will never date you," the girl that was with the man said, and mockingly laughed at Shanaya.

Shanaya looked down at her feet, avoiding eye contact. She tries her best not to show her weakness and stops herself from tearing up.

"And who gave you the right to decide whom I will date or not, huh?"

"Sidharth-" the man tried to clarify himself, but Sidharth beat him to it.

"Shanaya is someone you just can't help but fall in love with. How can someone not fall for her cute smile, her charming personality, her weird antics, or simply just her? She is one of those people who makes you feel like home just from the moment you've met her; makes you feel as if you've known them all your life. And not just that, she's also good academically. She has opinions about so many things. She loves to learn, she loves to read and even though she's shy, but when she sings, it's one of the most beautiful voices you've ever listened to. And how can I not date Shanaya when she loves playing over watch with me? Funny how she even gives me a tough competition and is even better than me. And have you even looked at her photography skills, huh? Everything she captures is an art. Everything she paints is a masterpiece, and she herself is no less than one." Sidharth said, "She's beautiful in every way possible and not just from the outside, but from the inside. Much more beautiful than all of you combined and I say that with full offense because even the mere thought of someone thinking that I would never date Shanaya makes me feel disgusted, and you think that I'm so called 'superior' or 'better' than her but I don't think there is anyone better than her to exist. She has the purest heart and one would be lucky to love her and loved by a girl like her. So don't even dare, from the next time, to say such a thing which can bring tears to her eyes because those are way too precious to be wasted on you, assholes. And for your kind information, she is the girl I want to be with the longest of time with because she means the most to me, so all of you should keep your dumb opinions, especially about me and my life to yourselves."

"Sidharth... I-I'm sorry," the man lowered his head and walked away from embarrassment, grabbing the girl's wrist.

Shanaya couldn't believe what Sidharth had just said. She stared at him with her mouth agape. Was this just a dream? She stood up and held

Sidharth's hand, trying to process if all of this was real. Sidharth looked at her with a warm smile, squeezing her hand comfortingly.

Sidharth pulled her closer with an expression which screamed as if he was proud to be with someone like Shanaya, and Shanaya just didn't know how to feel about it. She felt like crying, but for the first time it was not because she was sad, but these tears were the sign of how happy Sidharth had made her. And the way Sidharth had looked at her with those glowing eyes while tightening the hold of their intertwined hands, that was the moment she knew it was real and that maybe even Sidharth loved her the same way as she loved Sidharth.

Shanaya and Sidharth walked away hand in hand. Kiya left after checking on her and said that Shanaya should just skip the class, she'll make an excuse to the teacher for her. They were on their way back to their dorm.

"T-thank you." Shanaya said softly to him.

"You don't need to thank me shanu, I just stated facts back there." Sidharth smiled warmly at her, trying to lighten up the mood.

"I-I um didn't know you felt about me that way, I thought you liked someone else and were just really kind and see me as a good friend," Shanaya stopped in their tracks, looked at their intertwined hands with a soft blush on her cheeks, "I never knew you like me the same way I like you."

Sidharth furrowed his eyebrows, clearly confused. He doesn't know what Shanaya is talking about.

"Of course, I like you." Sidharth replied with a fond smile gracing his lips.

Shanaya looked at him wide eyed, "I-Is this a dream? If it is, I don't want to wake up from it," she chuckled.

"I have always wished for this day to come. For you to notice me and fall in love with me..." Shanaya trailed off, swallowing the lump that's forming in his throat.

Sidharth understood the situation now and was about to say that he just did it out of reflex, but before he could say anything, Shanaya talked again.

"I'm always the happiest when I'm with you, and I'm even happier now that I know you love me, too. You were the one that came without a warning, the one that I never knew I needed in my life. You made me feel different emotions and brought out various sides of me, I never knew existed," Shanaya looked at him with softness in her eyes, she lets go of their intertwined hands and held Sidharth's hands in hers, "I love you Sidharth and I'll be glad to be yours."

Sidharth stood there in silence, his head full of thoughts on how complicated all of this is. But he only knew one thing, that he can't break Shanaya's heart.

Sidharth just smiled at him and sighed, pulling Shanaya into a tight hug.

Sidharth didn't know what to feel about what Shanaya had just said. He didn't know how to react to Shanaya's love for him. He hadn't known what had gotten into him when he said all those words to the man, but he hated seeing tears in the older's eyes. Shanaya indeed did meant the most to him and she was his best friend and she indeed was the person he wanted to have for the longest time in his life. Of course, he wanted his best friend with him for the longest time; who wouldn't?

All the things he had said to Shanaya were all true, and he loved her as well, but it would be a lie if he said he was in love with her, too. Sidharth loved Shanaya, but not in the way she wanted Sidharth to love her. He couldn't love her that way when he already had someone else whom he liked that way, and especially when it was the day; he thought of asking his crush out. He couldn't love Shanaya that way. At the same moment, he thought of being with someone else and not her. Sidharth couldn't fall in love with Shanaya; at least not yet.

For a moment, he felt like he should have told Shanaya that it was all a misunderstanding and he wasn't really in love with her. And even though one would be lucky to fall in love with her, he didn't consider himself that lucky at all. But having seen Shanaya look genuinely so happy for the first time in a while, Sidharth didn't feel like breaking her heart and even though he was about to compromise with his own feelings for it, he was ready to do so.

He wasn't really in love with her but trying to falling in love felt like the best option seeing Shanaya smile like that. Smile in a way as if that moment had meant everything to her.

They always say that one should be with someone who loves them and not the one they love who doesn't love them back if given a choice and Sidharth thought maybe he should do that too? Falling in love with Shanaya wouldn't be so difficult, right? Even though he has only loved her platonically and never planned to change so. He saw Shanaya being so happy because of his overtime; it freaked him out a bit but Shanaya was happy and she could be happier with him, and he was more than happy to do so. To make Shanaya happy even if it wasn't where his own happiness stood.

Sidharth knew they both weren't in it for the same emotions anymore; the same feelings anymore.

It's sketchy but isn't sketch an art too? Isn't love and sacrifice an art too? Wasn't the happiness in Shanaya's eyes an art too? Even though art can be sad, it is still beautiful. And like every other art which is preserved, he will try to preserve this one too.

He'll try to fall in love too, if it could make Shanaya happy. And just maybe, he too could be happy by just seeing Shanaya happy.

Sidharth was up the whole night that day and by the time he finally got to sleep, his alarm sounded, waking him up. He was restless, and he was so out of it; he didn't notice the milk overflowing as he filled his glass.

"Shit!" Sidharth backed away, avoiding the spilled milk.

Shanaya looked at him with a worried expression on his face. "You, okay?"

"Yeah, just didn't get enough sleep."

"How about you take a rest for today? One absent won't harm your grades." Her voice was soothing and calm, rubbing Sidharth's back up and down comfortingly.

"I can't. I have an important exam coming, I can't dare to be absent from the lectures."

"Okay babe, but don't stress out too much hm?" Shanaya said, turning around to grab her cup of coffee.

Sidharth's ears rang at what Shanaya called to him. He stood still for a moment, taking it in and slowly realising that this is what he had agreed to yesterday. This is what the result of how he acted yesterday after hearing Shanaya's confession to him.

"Hey, take some rest during your vacant time here, okay?" She said once more, looking at him with her cup of coffee in her hands.

"Okay." Sidharth replied, staring at Shanaya's coffee.

"I'll head to school first? Your class doesn't start in 30 minutes, right?"

Sidharth just nodded and moved away to sit on the couch in their mini living room. Shanaya just observed him. She's kind of worried about Sidharth but, thought that it would be fine after. It was their first day as an official couple and she was more than happy on this day.

"I will text you later!! Take care baby, love you!" Shanaya said as she closed the door.

Sidharth sat there, watching the program on the television, but his thoughts wandered away. The last words Shanaya said were still echoing inside his head, making him confused if he was doing the right thing. But he's already here. He needs to stand for his actions and try his best to fall in love with his best friend. It's gonna be easy, right?

"Good morning, boyfie," Shanaya muttered, snuggling closer to Sidharth.

"Ah um, good morning to you too?" Sidharth said awkwardly and stiffened.

"Let's have breakfast baby, get up," Shanaya smiled brightly at him and got up. She pulled Sidharth up and gave him a good morning kiss on the cheek.

Sidharth didn't know how he should react. He quickly got up instead and gave her an awkward smile. He said nothing else and headed to the bathroom, while Shanaya went to the kitchen and cooked them a nice breakfast. Too engrossed in her perfect dream that turned into reality.

"What time is your class today?" Shanaya asked, intertwining her fingers with Sidharth's.

"In 30 minutes." Sidharth glanced at their hands and looked at her.

Shanaya stared at him with expectation, so he held her hand tighter. She looked away shyly with a faint smile on her lips. Sidharth sighed, letting himself try to get comfortable with the situation and constantly thinking, 'it's okay.'

"I'll see you after class?" Shanaya reached over and brushed through Sidharth's hair.

"My class ends a bit late, so you should go home first," Sidharth said with a subtle smile, grabbing Shanaya's wrist to stop her.

"Okay, I'll see you at home then." She flashed a sweet smile and planted a soft kiss on his cheek before saying goodbye.

Sidharth heaves a deep sigh, holding his cheek. Thinking that maybe it will get better in time and it's just awkward for now because they just started.

It was another day in their dorms. Shanaya was in the kitchen cooking for the both of them as she always had ever since they started going out. She loved cooking for Sidharth and seeing the smile on her face every time he tasted what she made.

"Do you want me to help?" Sidharth asked, taking a seat at the dining table.

Shanaya looked at him lovingly, "it's okay baby, I'm almost done."

It's kinda funny how Shanaya has been calling him by that pet name naturally, but whenever he tries to use that word, it gets caught in his throat and it never comes out, no matter how much he tries. He says nothing about it though, but Sidharth could feel that sometimes Shanaya calls him by that multiple times so she could hear it from him as well.

"Ta-da!! I made your favorite egg fried rice!" Shanaya said cheerfully and placed the food in front of him.

"Wow, thank you ba- Sha," Sidharth smiled at her with apologetic eyes that he can't call her what she wants him to.

But Shanaya doesn't mind and expects Sidharth to taste what she had made even more.

"I hope you'll like it." Shanaya bites her lower lip and takes a seat beside him.

She takes a spoonful and tries to feed Sidharth. "open up," she chuckles.

"It's okay, I can do it." Sidharth refuses and sees Shanaya's smile falter. He feels sorry and lets Shanaya feed him instead, earning a boxy smile from her.

Sidharth says nothing else and focuses on the taste of the food that Shanaya made. The older quietly waits for his reaction as she looks at him.

"This tastes so good," Sidharth says out loud, amazed. Truthfully, he didn't find it that good, rather it was bland, but he couldn't say that to her.

"Really???"

"Really, really," Sidharth shows her his bunny smile, "Thank you. I love this."

"You're welcome," Shanaya says with a wide smile, satisfied with Sidharth's reaction.

They continued eating together with Shanaya, occasionally showing him affection that is hard for Sidharth to reciprocate. But he tries his best to make Shanaya happy and feel the love that she deserves.

Sidharth leaned back comfortably on the couch. Shanaya sat beside him and looked at him, then looked back at the show on the television. It bore her to death and wanted the younger's attention.

"Let's go on a date?" Shanaya pouts. She hasn't really gone on a date with Sidharth ever since they became official.

"Huh? What date?" Sidharth replied, his eyes still glued in front of him.

"Um, well, I've always wanted to go on an ice cream date with you, and those other little cute dates..." Shanaya looked down at her hands.

Sidharth was gonna say that they've already done those before, but Shanaya stopped talking so he looked at her and found the older looking down with her cheeks red.

"Okay, when do you want to go?" Sidharth said, a small smile plastered on his face. He could never dare to deny Shanaya's request, especially when he sees her like that.

Shanaya looked up, smiling at him happily, that her eyes turned into crescents, and stood up.

"I wanna go now!!" Shanaya pulled Sidharth up with her.

"Hm, how about I choose your flavor and you choose mine?" Shanaya proposed, holding Sidharth's hand. She was looking at the ice cream flavors they had, but she couldn't decide.

Sidharth just nodded and smiled faintly at her. He felt kinda uneasy with holding Shanaya's hand, but he did his best not to show it.

"I pick strawberry flavor for you." Sidharth said as they chose the ice cream flavors.

"H-how did you know I like strawberry?" Shanaya turned away, her face flushing. "then um, cookies and cream for you."

Shanaya found it endearing how Sidharth pays attention to the little things that she didn't find important at all. Her favorite ice cream flavor, her favorite color, her favorite anime, her favorite restaurant and even her favorite movie. She thinks Sidharth is that interested in her, that he knows what she likes and what she doesn't like. Her thoughts fly over to thinking that Sidharth might have been in love with her since before he confessed, but just didn't tell her. She looks at Sidharth lovingly, the blush on her cheeks getting darker.

"Coffee or tea, ma'am? It's a free sample for our new menu." The friendly worker offered.

"Oh, 2 coffees please!" Shanaya said before intertwining her fingers with Sidharth's. She always loved how Sidharth's bigger hand fit perfectly with her.

"Coffee?"

"You like coffee, right?" Shanaya grinned at him.

Sidharth gave her a small smile. He may have preferred coffee years ago, but now, he actually likes tea more than coffee. But well, that just adds to another thing that he couldn't tell Shanaya.

Photography class full of discussions was Shanaya's least favorite thing about this class. She wanted to learn about pictures and how she should capture them. The tips and tricks that every photographer has that make the picture turn even more beautiful. She was already bored and her boyfriend was busy focusing on his notebook.

"Siddd," Shanaya pouted. She rested her head on the table, looking at him. Sidharth was busy scribbling in his notebook. Actually, none of them were listening to the instructor.

"Yeah?"

"Hold my hand." She outstretched her hand to Sidharth beside him.

Sidharth sighed and took her hand. Shanaya tightened her hold with a satisfied smile on her face. The people sitting behind them noticed and teased them about how cheesy they were making their relationship public like that.

"Shanaya and Sidharth." The instructor grabbed their attention.

"Congratulations. Even if public display of affection is allowed in this school, I still don't appreciate seeing it in my class, especially when I'm discussing in front."

With that, the couple earned cheers from the class and congratulations all over. Sidharth laughed mockingly at them while Shanaya looked down, flushed. It was not in Shanaya's plan to make them go public like that, but she couldn't say that she didn't like it. She liked everyone knowing that Sidharth is hers and Shanaya is Sidharth's only. She knew Sidharth was popular and girls had a crush on him, so she felt really loved that he chose her and everyone knew about it.

"Be sweet after my class. Pay attention for now."

"Yes, ma'am." They both said in unison.

After class, Shanaya clung onto Sidharth's arm as they walked around the campus. Every student, even teachers, that passed by looked at them, but it was no surprise. Almost everyone already expected for the both of them to end up together. They actually thought they were already in a relationship but were hiding it until the bullying incident happened. They always saw them together and noticed how Shanaya looked at Sidharth.

Sidharth said nothing and just let Shanaya do anything she wanted. His priority was Shanaya's happiness, and he was glad to see that she was.

Shanaya had been less clingy to Sidharth and almost everyone noticed. People asked questions. She only told them it's because they are trying to become more private now.

"Lovebirds!!" Kiya rushed to the two of them and gave them a flyer.

"What's this?" Shanaya curiously reads what's written on it and Sidharth peers over.

"It's a promo from the new cafe that opened. Free food for couples! I actually know the owner so he asked me to help promote and good thing I know a very lovey dovey couple," Kiya grinned.

"I don't know, Kiya, I still have a class later," Sidharth said skeptically.

Kiya gasped. "You never say no to free food, Sid. Anything wrong?"

"What's gotten into you?" Shanaya glanced at him, "Of course we will go, and I mean right now," she smiled at Kiya.

"Yes!! Okay, just bring that flyer then, I guess that's it?" Kiya chuckled, "I'll see you later!! I have to give out more flyers," she smiled at them and turned to leave.

"You're not serious, are you? You're gonna end up skipping class."

Shanaya just rolled her eyes at him with a playful smile on her lips and walked ahead. Sidharth caught up and held her hand without thinking. She blushed at the touch and tightened her hold.

Sidharth was spoiling her, encouraging her and loving her and, most importantly, believing in her. Sidharth was there with her as Shanaya fulfilled her dreams and won over her insecurities encouraging her in every step of the way. He was making her laugh when she felt down; he was making Shanaya fall in love with him every single day. Sidharth was patient with her. Even when she was being rude to him and pushing him away, she was making time for him, even when he didn't have to. He told her she's beautiful and made her feel special every passing second for even existing. Sidharth treated her gently and softly. He looked out for her when she couldn't for herself. He made Shanaya feel important and as if he was proud to be with someone like her. Sidharth was doing everything she had been craving for months.

"Hi!! Kiya told us to just show this to you?" Shanaya gave him the flyer.

"Oh! Another couple! This is making me feel even more single. Take a seat. I'll just serve the food to you."

Shanaya looked at Sidharth and stared at him, looking around the place. It was a small and cute cafe with white and red colors around it with strawberry accents that seem to be the cafe's highlight. She observed Sidharth that looked just like a kid, amazed at the interior and at how everything was brand new. She sat across from him and when the younger made eye contact with her; she looked away and busied herself with her mobile phone.

"Here you go! I only serve desserts for now since it's already 2pm. Enjoy the desserts, lovers." The owner set down the tray of cake and ice cream on the table and slightly bowed to them.

"Oh, it's strawberry." Shanaya said, surprised.

"Your favorite."

Shanaya cleared her throat and tried to take a spoonful. "I wonder if it's good."

"Mmm it is." Sidharth cut a small part from the slice of cake and shoved it in his mouth, licking his lips.

"The ice cream is good too." Shanaya said with her mouth full.

Sidharth noticed the ice cream stain on the corner of Shanaya's lips. He leaned in closer and wiped it with his thumb unconsciously. "Uh, there was ice cream."

Shanaya, stunned, just stared at him for a while and looked down. It's unfair how her heart still beats for Sidharth after everything he had done. It's unfair how she still melts at the sweet little gestures that he does when it probably doesn't matter to the younger. When they walk hand in hand, it feels like nothing can hurt her. Every time when she's with Sidharth she wants it more, she wants all of it. The pointless bickering, the long walks, the late-night conversations, the good morning greetings. She wants the cute pictures with him, to make food for him, to call him baby, the wrestling, the cuddling, even the fights and maybe just everything. It's unfair how every time they say good bye, she misses him more. And every passing moment, she just loves him a little more than she did before. It's unfair how Sidharth is just being Sidharth and Shanaya can't help but be in love with him.

She shook her head, clearing her thoughts, and continued eating. She takes a quick glance at Sidharth who was looking at the people that come in through the door and sees a strawberry was left on his plate.

"Won't you eat that?" Shanaya pointed at the strawberry with her spoon.

"You can have it. I know that's your favorite part of the cake." Sidharth said like it's just nothing, but it's everything to her.

Shanaya tightened her grip around her spoon and collected herself. She took the strawberry and popped it inside her mouth, telling herself that this was real and Sidharth was her.

Shanaya saw Sidharth on the couch with his legs propped up on the coffee table and chips in his hands. Shanaya sighed and smiled fondly. Sidharth was watching the iron man again. Another 'stay in' weekend for them that Shanaya didn't really mind. She loved spending time with the younger no matter where they were. But Sidharth had an important group project to work on in the afternoon.

Shanaya sat beside him and slowly lied down, laying her head on Sidharth's lap. Sidharth sat up, clearly uncomfortable with the position, but she was too giddy to notice.

"Gimme." She looked up at Sidharth and then at the chips in his hand, pouting.

Sidharth tried to give the bag of chips to Shanaya, but the older shook her head instead and opened her mouth.

"Feed me," another pout.

Sidharth just complies and placed a piece in Shanaya's mouth. She munched on the chip and smiled sweetly at him. If they weren't in this relationship, he wouldn't have minded all of this, but this was different. He already knew Shanaya feels different. They both continued watching the movie until it ended.

"Baby," Shanaya sat up and clung to Sidharth, "do you really have to go?"

"Yup, I'll be back immediately, though." He pulled away from her gently and stood up.

"Aww okay. Text me when you get there?"

"Of course. See you later." Sidharth opened the door as Shanaya gave him a quick kiss on the cheek. He just smiled in return.

Sidharth made a quick text to Shanaya that he's on his way home and placed his phone in his pocket. He passed by a captivating candy shop with all of its bright colors and delish displays. Sidharth went inside to look. His doe's eyes widened as he inspected the place. It always fascinated him with things like these; until he spotted a strawberry shaped container with strawberry candies inside. He smiled at himself and thought how Shanaya would love that and use the container for storage.

"That's our strawberry berry sir, it's the only one left." The staff smiled at him politely.

"I'll take it."

"Do you want it wrapped, sir? It's free service."

"Really?? I'd like that, thank you." Sidharth smiled back.

The staff comes back and hands him a pretty and petite box. Sidharth thanked him once more and headed home.

He knocked on their door once and it flew open, revealing Shanaya on the other side, lunging at him.

"I missed you." Shanaya hugs him tightly.

"I wasn't gone that long." Sidharth laughed awkwardly, with his hands at the sides.

"Still," Shanaya gives him the puppy eyes that lands on the box he's bringing with his one hand, "what's that?"

Sidharth looked at the box and held it in front of her. "I found a candy shop when I was on my way here and thought you'd like this."

Shanaya's eyes sparkled and took the box, placing it on their coffee table in the living room. Sidharth follows her and sees Shanaya slowly opening it.

"Omg, I love this!!" Shanaya beams at him.

She stood up and placed Sidharth's hand on her. "Thank you, baby." She softly gave him a peck on the lips. "I love you so much."

Sidharth stood still at that and gave her a slight smile. He didn't expect that kind of reaction from Shanaya and he didn't even know what to feel about it. Shanaya pulled him into a tight hug and he sighed, not knowing what else to do but just resign.

Shanaya woke up and noticed that Sidharth wasn't beside her. She got up and took a peek at the kitchen to find him whistling and cooking. Shanaya smiled fondly and stretched her arms lazily as she walked quietly to where her boyfriend was. She snaked her arms around Sidharth's waist from the back.

"Good morning, my baby." Shanaya said, burying her face in the crook of Sidharth's neck, breathing him in.

Sidharth was startled, but he kept himself undisturbed in a way that Shanaya wouldn't recognize. He still felt uncomfortable with all of this set up between the two of them, even if it's already been months.

"Morning," he replies, pulling Shanaya gently away from him, "you might get burnt. Go take a seat." Sidharth smiled at him slightly.

Shanaya pouts and nods. She took a seat and waited for Sidharth. Sidharth was wearing a black tank top with black comfortable boxers, and his hair was disheveled all over. He looked incredibly hot. Shanaya stared at him lustfully, like she's ready to devour him, licking her lips as Sidharth got closer.

"You're hungry?" Sidharth asked, oblivious.

"I'm hungry for you. Can I have my morning kiss?" Shanaya pouted, making eye contact with Sidharth.

It was not like Sidharth had never kissed Shanaya. He had done it before, maybe once, when Shanaya really begged for him to and he always avoided it, which came to where the older ignored him the whole day. It resulted in Shanaya crying that night, talking about her insecurity and how she feels unwanted. Sidharth kissed her plump lips softly that night, comforting her she's so much better than what she thinks of himself.

Sidharth sighed. He placed their breakfast on the table and gave Shanaya a warm smile. "Maybe later."

Shanaya pouted even more, but nodded. Sidharth sits beside her, takes a spoonful of the kimchi fried rice that he made and feeds Shanaya, trying to make up for the kiss. Shanaya's pout slowly turns into a boxy smile. Her bad mood always turns the opposite whenever Sidharth does something for her.

Sidharth woke up earlier than usual. He could feel his body sore from the stiff position and was gonna move to the side when he felt something heavy on his chest. He looked down and saw Shanaya's sleeping face. She looked so at peace. He didn't want to wake her up, so he tried to go back to sleep when the older moved a bit, making a small space free for him to go.

Sidharth got up gently and occasionally looked back at Shanaya. He sat on the couch, staring blankly at the coffee that he just made. It's been 6 months since they became a couple.

Shanaya had always been a best friend to Sidharth - the one who had been there for him from the very beginning, the one who handled him at his worst, the one who knew all his secrets and the one with whom he could be his absolute best and worst.

Every time he looked at her, all he saw was love and admiration, and maybe some hope. She would look at him with feelings and Sidharth would avoid her gaze; hoping it was all in his head and Shanaya wasn't actually in love with him. He repeatedly told himself that it can't be true and that it's impossible. That they were just best off friends. That they were terrible as lovers because Sidharth had never looked at her romantically; even when he wanted to try, he somehow just couldn't. Shanaya was the girl who kept it together, pretending that being in an unrequited love didn't hurt her, but looking at those eyes he knew it did. Shanaya tried to find happiness in Sidharth's happiness, and smiled whenever he talked about Yoona, even though she was terribly breaking from the inside.

Shanaya is the girl who showered him with compliments. "You're the best and perfect in my eyes." Sidharth knows he's not; he just can't be after probably breaking Shanaya's heart, and maybe he still is. Shanaya was everything anyone could ever ask for and Sidharth should have ended up with her, but his goddamn stupid heart couldn't find it in himself to love her romantically.

Even after trying for over months, he just couldn't and now he was tired. Tired of pretending to be in love when he was not, tired of hearing Shanaya say that "being with you makes me the happiest," tired of bearing the smile that doesn't hold a meaning when it should, tired of spitting lies because he was too cowardly to speak the truth. Tired of seeing Shanaya believing something which isn't true.

Sidharth had gone into the relationship thinking it would be like any other arranged marriage and he would eventually fall in love with Shanaya. He tried his best at it, too. He moved on from his stupid crush on Yoona and genuinely tried to fall in love with Shanaya. Sidharth hated the people who said falling love was one of the easiest things and that it happens naturally. If it was so easy, then why was Sidharth having so much difficulty in falling in love with his best friend? Why was it so difficult to fall in love with Shanaya? That Shanaya, whom Sidharth believed, owned the purest heart.

In the 6 months of being together with Shanaya, he may not have fallen in love with her, but he seemed to have hated himself. Hate himself for hurting Shanaya and hate himself for making Shanaya believe something which wasn't true and probably wouldn't ever be. The relationship, which was supposed to be beautiful, now felt like it was suffocating him; consuming him in the worst ways it could.

He couldn't make himself feel like doing it anymore, it just didn't feel right. Shanaya's love had overwhelmed him now and a lot of times make him feel uncomfortable. Sidharth hated the fact that being with Shanaya had felt uncomfortable. Sidharth knew this was it. He couldn't do this anymore. He needed an escape and let the reality sink in.

It was his fault that he couldn't make himself fall in love, right? Well then, he deserved a punishment too, or so he thought. Sidharth couldn't fall in love with Shanaya, but maybe Shanaya could fall out of it, perhaps even hate him for it. He was gonna make sure that Shanaya would hate him because she deserved someone a lot better than Sidharth. Shanaya deserved true love and not a mere pretense of it. Shanaya deserved happiness and not Sidharth for it.

Months back he gave up on his feelings just for Shanaya's happiness and once again he was ready to do so, but this time he knew there was no turning back or a happy ending to it. So, what if Sidharth would be hated by the one who meant the most to him? So, what if he would be hated by Shanaya? Once again, he really didn't care about himself, but all he cared about was Shanaya's happiness and he was ready to give up anything for it. Maybe even their relationship and the most important thing to him- their friendship.

"Sid?" Shanaya said, touching the empty side of the bed.

"Hey," Sidharth said softly. Shanaya stood up and headed towards him.

"Good morning, happy 6 months to us." Shanaya wrapped her arms around Sidharth's neck and sat on his lap.

Sidharth holds Shanaya, his hand on the small of her back and just smiles at her, a sad glimmer in his eyes that Shanaya is too blind to see.

It was a fresh day in their dorm. They just finished with their exams and it was finally almost their summer break. Shanaya just woke up minutes ago and was looking for Sidharth as she always had these days. And the younger was on the couch, staring blankly at the wall.

Shanaya rubbed her eyes. Pouting, she went into the living room lazily. She saw Sidharth sitting on the couch, smiled and laced her arms around him from the back.

"Mm, good morning," Shanaya whispered with a husky morning voice, placing a soft kiss on Sidharth's cheek.

"Oh morning," Sidharth said, surprised, the gesture bringing him back into reality. He looked at Shanaya with a blank expression on his face and looked away. Shanaya let go and plopped on the couch sitting beside him.

"You should've woken me up when you did!!" Shanaya said, pouting.

"You were sleeping so soundly, I couldn't." Sidharth replied without even looking at her, and turned on the television. Shanaya's pout slowly turned into a smile upon hearing that.

"Should we go out to have breakfast?" Shanaya asked, looking at the younger.

"We could just have some bread and jam, it's fine," Sidharth said, but in his mind he actually thought that it's not actually breakfast when it's past 10 in the morning, but more like brunch.

Shanaya goes to the kitchen humming, making bread and jam sandwiches for the both of them. Sidharth doesn't move from where he is and focuses on the show in front of him. His mind drifted off somewhere else as Shanaya gave him his sandwich and settled beside him.

"Sid baby, look." Shanaya showed Sidharth her phone that displayed a new restaurant that opened up just a few blocks from their dorm.

Sidharth looked at it for a bit and replied, "oh that's great," clearly uninterested.

"I thought maybe we could go today? It's just near and we're free today." Shanaya bit her lower lip anxiously. She could feel Sidharth's sudden shift of mood and during times like these, he's usually stressed out and just wanted to be left on his own.

"Not now Sha, you know I'm still busy with something," Sidharth said without looking at her.

"Oh, okay." She replied disheartened and proceeded to just scroll through the internet. She contemplates maybe Sidharth is just tired from the exams and all.

The silence was deafening between the two of them, with only their breaths and the program on the television making sounds. Shanaya's eyes light up at the text message she received from Kiya saying that she'd want to meet the lovers for a coffee date, maybe in the late afternoon.

"Kiya texted me just now. She wanted to see us and maybe grab some coffee?" Shanaya carefully asked.

"Kiya Di? Tell her that. Of course we'll go. Just say the name of the place and we'll be there," Sidharth replied cheerfully. He hasn't hung out with Kiya outside their classes since they were busy and there was always Shanaya.

Shanaya avoids his gaze, not knowing what to say, and wonders what made his boyfriend's mood change once again. But she decides not to mind it at all and replies to Kiya that they'll be there.

"Shanu!! Sid!! Over here!!" Kiya raised her hand, trying to get their attention. She was sitting at a table for 3 people, just perfect for them.

"Kiyaie!!" Shanaya grabbed Sidharth's hand and went to where Kiya was seated.

"Hi Kiya Di!! I missed hanging out with you," Sidharth said with a bright smile as they sat down.

"Aww I missed you too Sid," Kiya replied, her eyes turning into crescents.

Shanaya cleared her throat, making it obvious that she's kind of left out of the conversation and smiled at Kiya.

"I missed you too Sha!! It's been a while," Kiya said.

"Got busy with exams." She replies, a small smile plastered on her face.

Kiya nods, "so anything you'd like? I'd go buy it for all of us."

"Oh, 2 iced coffees for us." Shanaya smiled proudly, thinking how cheesy it is that they both had the same taste.

"Actually, I'll have iced tea," Sidharth interjects.

Shanaya looked at him surprised. "I thought you liked coffee?"

"Not really, I prefer tea." Sidharth smiled at her. He wasn't gonna pretend anymore.

"So, um an iced coffee and an iced tea," Shanaya looked at Kiya with a tight smile.

"Okay, I'll be right back." Kiya got up and headed to the counter.

"Why haven't you told me you preferred tea over coffee?" Shanaya asked, looking down at her hands.

"You didn't ask me." Sidharth shrugs.

"You could have told me???" Shanaya shoots him a look.

"I never thought it was important." Sidharth looked back at her, his eyes cold.

"Here you go!" Kiya sets down the tray of drinks for them. Shanaya and Sidharth both look away from each other.

"Thank you, Ki." Sidharth gives her a warm smile and takes the iced tea.

"Thanks." Shanaya also takes her drink.

Kiya could feel the tension between the lovers and tried to break the ice.

"How have you two been?" Kiya asked, taking a sip from her drink.

"We're okay." Sidharth replied nonchalantly.

"Um, yeah, we're fine," Shanaya adds.

"That's good. You two are so inseparable!! Everyone knows that you two have been together for months now. They even ask me what it's like to third wheel you both." Kiya chuckled.

Shanaya smiled shyly at that. She had always wanted to have that kind of relationship that everyone knows about.

"How was your exam, Kiya Di?" Sidharth asked, changing the topic.

"Have you answered that last part in the back??? I didn't see it!!" Kiya ranted and talked about how clumsy she was.

Shanaya just listened to the both of them talk, occasionally laughing at the conversation but never really joining in. Her mind was too preoccupied with what Kiya said, and her heart fluttered with it, forgetting about what happened between Sidharth and her just moments ago. It was the first time in years that someone made her feel important - feel loved. Sidharth really made her feel that. It made Shanaya a little secure, but she knew it was too selfish of her. What had changed was that suddenly Shanaya wasn't feeling it anymore. That she was missing having that feeling of being loved all the more again. For a moment when she thought that everything was perfect, it seemed that moment had broken and nothing seemed to be perfect anymore. In fact, she could feel a slight crack increasing more and more. For, the first time in a while she was scared that one day Sidharth would get tire of her or he would want things which Shanaya can't give and she just won't be good enough. Scared that one day she would wake up and nothing won't be the same again and Sidharth would not love her anymore. That he's gonna get sick of her craziness, her constant need of reassurance, of not being left by him - her Sidharth.

She's scared that Sidharth would get bored and would want to be with someone new. Someone who deserves to be with him and not some who's insecure to be left by the only person she would do anything to not get dropped by. She's scared that one day Sidharth is going to see her the way she sees herself. Shanaya feared letting that happen. For the first time since she met Sidharth, she was scared of losing him.

Shanaya was in a great mood today. They were finally gonna go on a date after days of being too busy for each other because of exams and prior engagements.

Shanaya was staring at Sidharth from head to toe as the younger combed his hair in front of their huge mirror. She smiled fondly at the view in front of her.

It's true that some things never change. Their friends were still supportive, as they were at the start, along with Nikhil and Shalini. All of them knew about Shanaya's feelings for Sidharth were more than just friends before Shanaya did. She was so thankful for them and she couldn't imagine being what she was today without them by their side.

What changed even more was how Sidharth became colder to her. The same Sidharth who would do everything to make her smile, even if she was in the same dull mood. But today, Shanaya could feel Sidharth farther from her. Seems like there's a first for everything.

"I'll see you at the restaurant?" Sidharth said as he grabbed his jacket.

"Okay." Shanaya leaned a bit to give him a kiss on the cheek, but before she could, Sidharth moved away and got out of the door.

Shanaya sighed and smiled sadly. She thinks that it's okay. Sidharth is still stressed out with that last project and they'll have a date later, anyway.

Sidharth had to visit Kiya to finish their project that was to be submitted by the end of the week, then it was finally summer break. Kiya offered Shanaya to go as well, but she didn't want to intervene, especially when there were other people she didn't know.

Shanaya arrived a bit earlier than their planned time thinking that Sidharth might wait for her if she was gonna be late. But she had already texted Sidharth a few times, asking where he was or how much longer he was gonna take, but there was no reply. She even tried calling him, but she couldn't reach his number. She was getting worried with every second that passed by that she called Kiya, who was with Sidharth the last time she checked.

"Ki, are you still with Sidharth?" Shanaya asked worriedly.

"Sidharth? No Sha, he left an hour ago and was rushing to head at some place. Why?" Kiya said on the other line.

"We have a date today and I've been waiting here for an hour already, but he's not replying to my texts and I can't reach his number either. I'm worried." She said, resting her head against her hand.

"I'll try calling him, but maybe he's on his way there. Don't worry too much." Kiya tried to reassure her.

"Okay, thank you Kiya." Shanaya said and ended the call.

After waiting for another 30 minutes, Shanaya was about to give up and go home when Sidharth entered the restaurant and rushed up to their table.

"Hey, I'm sorry I'm late. There was heavy traffic." Sidharth said and sat on the seat across from Shanaya.

"Why didn't you reply to my texts? And why can't I reach you?" Shanaya asked with a frustrated tone in her voice.

"Oh, my phone died on the way here," Sidharth said nonchalantly.

"Okay," Shanaya sighed, "let's order?" She just pretends that she didn't wait for him for an hour and a half, getting worried about what happened to him.

"Sure," Sidharth replied with a slight smile.

Sidharth knew that what he did had hurt Shanaya but he wasn't lying when he said his phone died and about the traffic, but he may have gotten a bit more late because he was spacing out thinking about all of this. He avoids the sad look on Shanaya's face in front of him and convinces himself that he's doing the right thing. That if Shanaya stays by his side any longer, she would get hurt more than she already is in Sidharth's presence.

Shanaya gave him a reassuring smile. She was just glad that Sidharth could make it and she hides the pain in her eyes.

As the food that they ordered arrived, they talked about Sidharth's project and how it went. It was all about school and never about the two of them. The dessert served brought back a memory from their past though, and Shanaya had a wonderful one at that.

"Oh, red velvet cake!!" Sidharth exclaimed as his face lit up and showed a wide smile.

"I missed having this," Shanaya said and takes a spoonful into her mouth.

"This tastes so good," Sidharth said, savoring the flavor.

"Especially after a tiring class," Shanaya chuckled, "remember when we used to have this all the time when you haven't moved in at the dorm yet?" She says, reminiscing about their memories.

"Those were the best red velvet cake I've ever tasted," Sidharth said and continued eating.

"You kept on feeding me too and always kept on looking at my reaction." Shanaya smiled fondly and blushed.

"Did I?" Sidharth asked, bewildered.

"You did. Will you feed me now?" Shanaya smiled, looking at him.

"We're in public, Sha, and I can't just do that suddenly," Sidharth replied as he finished the cake.

Sidharth hated to act this way around Shanaya when she didn't deserve it at all. He knew Shanaya was the right one for him. Shanaya was perfect in every sense - loving, caring, empathetic, understanding, kind and a good person.

Sidharth thought even if at some point if he fell in love with Shanaya, he surely didn't deserve to be with someone like her. Shanaya was everything anybody could ask for in a girl, yet somehow, she fell in love with a mess like Sidharth.

Shanaya was someone that still texted him when he hasn't replied for hours, watches him give other people attention while he ignores her even though she hated what he did, handles all the bullshit he throws at her. He wants to thank her, and say he loves her, and let her know he doesn't take her for granted and he never wants to let her go because he will never find someone like her ever again because people like her are just so hard to find.

But even though Shanaya was the one he should fall in love with, he was not ready to accept it. He wants everything with Shanaya, but he doesn't know the bridge to the other side and that's why he should leave. Because the worst part was, he was losing his best friend and he couldn't even tell his best friend about it.

"Right," Shanaya sighed, gave him a small smile, and finished hers. Things like these shouldn't matter at all. It's true that it was months ago and they were different now, but it still stung a bit to hear that from the one that you never thought you'd hear it from.

That short conversation about their past made Shanaya feel like it was finally a date and not some school matter. Sidharth was rather silent after that and on their way home, he just slept in the car. When they arrived home, Sidharth stayed up all night to work on the final editing of their project and left Shanaya on the bed alone again.

Shanaya understands. They went on a date today anyway, so Sidharth already gave her even a little of his time. Shanaya convinces herself that it shouldn't hurt her. Sidharth is just doing his part for their group and for the future. Shaking her head of his thoughts, she hugs Sidharth's pillow and goes into a deep slumber.

Sidharth felt sick and could actually feel his heart break seeing Shanaya so broken. And what hurt the most was that he was the reason behind it. He didn't know how to look at Shanaya like this and even though she was the one he wanted to be with until the end; it was time to walk away. This didn't hurt him any less.

Sidharth went to school earlier today, which is why Shanaya woke up without him in the dorm. Shanaya texted him where he was and received a dull reply of "school." She sighed. Sidharth was really being different from the usual, and she didn't know why.

Shanaya got up and prepared herself to set off for her class. She was not in the mood to go, but she had to, of course.

She didn't pay any attention to class that she didn't notice when it ended. Shanaya was on her way to the library when she saw Sidharth. Her face brightened up in an instant and rushed to where he was until she saw him with Yoona. Her smiling face turned into a frown as she got near them and heard a bit of their conversation.

"...thanks for the cake, Yoona."

"Of course, Sid, I should be the one thanking you," Yoona replied shyly.

"But you didn't have to." Sidharth said, smiling at her.

"It wasn't even enough."

"It is Yoon-"

"Baby!! Here you are!!" Shanaya interrupted their conversation and held Sidharth's hand. "Oh! You must be Yoona?"

"Yes, I guess Sidharth talked about me? You're Shanaya right?" Yoona said, a warm smile on her lips.

"Yup, his girlfriend." Shanaya said proudly, smiling.

Sidharth let go of their hands and raised his eyebrows. "I thought you had a class?"

"It just ended a while ago."

"Um, I'll leave you two? I have a class in a few minutes. Nice meeting you Shanaya, see you around Sid." Yoona smiled and left them alone.

"What is your problem?" Sidharth looked at her, his eyebrows furrowed.

"Nothing??"

"Then why did you intervene in our conversation??!?"

"I'm sorry I just wanted to-"

"Wanted to what? Let everyone know you own me? Everyone already knows. You could've at least tried to respect our conversation and not butt in." Sidharth said harshly and walked away.

Shanaya bit her lower lip and heaved a deep sigh. It was the first time Sidharth snapped at her and even if she didn't want to admit it, what Sidharth said was true. She was being rude for no apparent reason except for being jealous of Yoona when she shouldn't be. Sidharth chose her after all, and she was his girlfriend, not anyone else. Shanaya collected herself and caught up to Sidharth.

"I'm sorry," Shanaya grabbed Sidharth's wrist, making him stop and look at her, "I-I just got jealous."

"There's nothing to be jealous of, just so you know."

"I know," Shanaya said apologetically and looked down.

Sidharth looked at her, "it's fine, I'll get going. I have a class in 5 minutes."

Sidharth then left after that, leaving Shanaya still guilty but stopped dwelling on it. She rushed to her next class and sent a text to Sidharth saying sorry. Sidharth replied after a few minutes, saying that it's okay and she should stop. Shanaya smiled at that and felt at ease.

Sidharth had been avoiding Shanaya's sweet gestures to him since then. He thinks Shanaya notices it too, but just acts the same, or not. Sidharth hasn't been sleeping in their bed as well. He tries to make the distance obvious until Shanaya asks him about it, but she doesn't.

"Will you sleep in our bed tonight?" Shanaya searches for Sidharth's eyes, trying to find an answer.

"Maybe. I just unintentionally fall asleep on the couch when I've been playing all night. It's not like I'm doing it on purpose." Sidharth reasoned out.

'Why are you lying to me?' Shanaya thinks, but says nothing. She then asks herself why would Sidharth even lie to her over such a silly thing and smiled softly.

"I just missed you. You haven't been sleeping in our bed these days and you used to sleep there no matter what," Shanaya says, looking at the floor.

"Okay, I'll sleep there tonight but let's not fight over this, alright?" Sidharth says with a smile which quite didn't reach his eyes and heads to the kitchen.

Shanaya resigned quietly and sat on the couch, clutching her heart tightly, hoping that the pain would be gone soon.

That night, Sidharth fulfilled what he said and slept on the bed, facing away from Shanaya. Shanaya wrapped her arms around Sidharth tightly as if she's scared of waking up without beside her until she fell asleep.

Sidharth didn't resist Shanaya that night and just let her be, telling himself that it's alright and it will be over soon.

Shanaya woke up at dawn with the sky still dark outside, the moon illuminating from the window hitting Sidharth's face, making his features sharper and more beautiful. Shanaya looks at him with a softness in her eyes, brushing Sidharth's hair off his face. It's supposed to feel warm beside him in the bed compared to those moments when he wasn't there, but it was the opposite. Shanaya felt colder with his presence.

It's finally their summer break. Shanaya had been waiting for this time to come so she could spend more time with Sidharth without interruptions. She missed her baby and thought that maybe they could go back to how they used to be.

"Hello?" Sidharth picked up his phone and said on the other line. Shanaya looked at him, not expecting someone to call.

"Nikhil bhaiya!! You want me to visit home today?" Sidharth looked into Shanaya's eyes and saw them sparkle, excited from what she heard.

Shanaya nodded her head almost immediately, and pointed at herself, mouthing a "tell bhaiya I will come too" at him.

"Okay bhaiya, I'll be there by the afternoon. Bye." Sidharth hung up.

"You didn't tell him I'll go with you?" Shanaya asked, looking at Sidharth.

"He already knows you are. We'll be there in the afternoon." Sidharth replied, avoiding his gaze.

Shanaya blushed a bit at what Sidharth said. It felt like they were already in a package. It was not like it was the first time, but she still found it cute and warm, unlike how Sidharth was towards her these days.

There was silence all throughout the way and Sidharth could slightly feel Shanaya trying to hide her sadness, but didn't speak about it.

"Sid!!" Shalini opened the door and hugged Sidharth.

"Oh Shalini Di!" Sidharth hugged her back with a big smile on his face. Shanaya looked at them fondly.

"Shanu!! I haven't seen you since forever." Shalini gave Shanaya a hug, too.

"Me too, di, how have you been?" Shanaya replied, slowly pulling away from the embrace.

"I'm doing great, especially with Nikhil." Shalini winked at them and laughed.

Sidharth just shakes his head, a smile plastered on his face and Shanaya laughed with Shalini. Nikhil placed his head on Shalini's shoulders, checking to see who was on the door since it's been minutes since she was there.

"Oh, Sid!! Why didn't you let them in?" Nikhil hit Shalini's shoulder playfully and opened the door wider to let them in.

"How are you two? You haven't visited us for months," Nikhil asked as they sat down on the couch in the living room.

"We're fine bhaiya," Sidharth replies indifferently.

"We're good Nikhil bhaiya, and I guess you two are doing well?" Shanaya said, faking a smile.

"Too well," Shalini smirks.

"They didn't need to know that Shalu," Nikhil glared at her, "I cleaned your room, Sid. You could sleep over today if you want with Shanaya, of course."

"Thanks, bhaiya," Sidharth says, smiling.

"Have you been taking care of Shanaya?" Nikhil asks, looking at the two of them. Shalini was in the kitchen getting some water for herself and some snacks.

"She... she can take care of herself bhaiya," Sidharth smiles slightly and avoids his gaze.

"That's right bhaiya, I can take care of myself," Shanaya laughs awkwardly.

Sidharth went upstairs to his room and Shanaya followed. When they finally went inside, Shanaya immediately plopped onto the bed, staring at the ceiling.

"You can stay here for now. I have to run some errands for Nikhil bhaiya," Sidharth says, looking at Shanaya, not expecting any reply, and leaves the room.

Shanaya closed his eyes shut and remembered how different it was back then. How Sidharth always took care of her, even with the littlest things and never found it tiring.

Shanaya curled in on herself and felt her heart break at the memory.

"Sha? Are you asleep?" Sidharth asks as he sits down on the chair near his bed.

"Can I take a walk in your garden? I kinda miss it," Shanaya says, standing up. Grabbing her jacket, and heads outside. Sidharth can only sigh at the sight of the door closing shut.

Shanaya didn't know what to feel. She didn't even know what she wanted to feel anymore. Shanaya didn't know if she really even wanted to know why Sidharth was behaving the way he was. She just couldn't figure out how things were anymore. It's like he suddenly didn't even want what she had worked so hard for getting. What she wanted was an escape because maybe, just maybe, she already knew the answer to all her questions but was too afraid to let it sink in. To have all things make sense.

Shanaya found herself hoping that all of this was just a lucid dream and when she finally wakes up, everything would still be the same. Everything would be back to how it used to be again.

That when she wakes up, Sidharth would be right beside her, telling her that everything is okay and he loves her. That Sidharth would kiss her tears away because all this feels like a very ugly nightmare. An ugly nightmare, which she hates being a part of. An ugly nightmare where she just can't figure who this new person is because Sidharth would never treat her this way. Because her Sidharth would do anything to even spend the shortest of the time with her, not like the one now who keeps on running away from her.

She felt empty; void of every emotion that she had ever felt. It felt like losing, but losing something she never really had. She felt like saving, but saving something which was already lost. She felt like crying, but the tears won't just come out. Shanaya felt like singing, but nothing she could think of. She wanted her Sidharth, but not the person Sidharth was now.

At one point, she was feeling a lot of things and at another, nothing at all; it was numb. The coexistence of contradictory emotions was messing up her mind. She kept thinking of reasons, but there were simply none. Or maybe the ones she didn't wanna acknowledge, not yet.

Shanaya sniffs, feeling the cold air in the garden as she got lost in her thoughts. She held her jacket around herself tighter and headed back inside the house. Taking a glance at Sidharth in the living room, she finds her heart ache and slowly heads upstairs to the younger's room.

♡

Despite Shanaya feeling the change, she doesn't want to face it, instead she tries everything that she did in the past that she thinks made Sidharth fall for her before, and that it may bring back some spark.

Shanaya started her plan today and the first thing she was gonna do is to cook Sidharth's favorite food. Sidharth loved her cooking so much before and it's been ages since she last made it.

Shanaya headed to the kitchen and found Shalini drinking a cup of warm coffee. Nikhil was in the living room, watching the early news on television.

"You're up early. Where's Sidharth?" Shalini asks, taking a sip from his coffee.

"He's asleep, I'm gonna cook di." Shanaya grins, wearing an apron.

"For Sidharth? Why? He doesn't wanna eat again?"

"No special occasion. I just missed cooking for him." Shanaya smiles slightly and begins cooking.

"Alright, I'll be in the living room with Nikhil. Call me if you need help." Shalini placed the cup in the sink and left Shanaya alone in the kitchen.

"Okay, I think this should do it," Shanaya says to herself proudly, finishing up.

Shanaya carefully transferred the dish into a bowl and placed it in a tray. She's planning to surprise Sidharth and bring it to him in his room.

Shanaya knocked on the door thrice and turned the knob. Sidharth was sitting on the chair facing the computer, and he turned around to see Shanaya, tray in hand, and the smell of the egg fried rice circulating in the room.

"Egg fried rice?" Sidharth asks, eyebrows furrowed.

"Your favorite." Shanaya replied, smiling. She placed the tray on Sidharth's desk.

"What's the occasion?" Sidharth looked at her and then at the bowl of egg fried rice.

"Nothing. I thought that you might have missed it." Shanaya gave him a small smile.

"Thank you, but I'm not hungry. I'll eat later." Sidharth smiled back at her and faced the monitor.

"You won't try it?" She asked, his voice low.

"It's fine. I already know it's good." Sidharth remarked, and continued working.

"Okay, enjoy." She said and with a sad smile on her face, she left the room.

It wasn't the reaction that she expected, but at least Sidharth complimented her on cooking a bit. That counts for something, right?

Sidharth always loved what Shanaya cooked. It is probably one of the best he had ever tasted. He would always hug Shanaya and tell her how much he loved her cooking, but this time he couldn't, as it would go against his plans. Every time the older would cook something for him and he found himself finding it out of the world and asking for more and more. It was maybe because Shanaya cooked it with a lot of sincerity and love and she was a good cook or simply because Sidharth had a personal bias when it came to her cooking. Whatever it was, he would choose Shanaya's cooking over any restaurant food any day, even when it was bland at certain times.

Even today he was dying inside to taste it and shower her with compliments, as he always does, but he didn't. He just complimented it to be good already. Sidharth hated doing all this, and what he hated even more was to see her sad. He wished he could see her smile, but alas, to eventually make Shanaya happy, he had to make her a bit sad now, even though doing it was killing him from the inside.

He decided to taste it when Shanaya would be gone, but now he really couldn't because he couldn't hurt her anymore.

Shanaya was bored and didn't know what to do. Sidharth was asleep in his bed and she didn't want to wake him up. She decided to play games, but after a while; she got bored and thought of cleaning the dorm. After she was done cleaning and arranging everything, She realised she still had a lot of time in her hands and arranged her closet as well. As she was arranging them, she came across a hoodie which wasn't really her own but had a lot of memories associated with it. She held it tightly and she could still smell the faint scent of Sidharth's perfume. She always loved his scent, and she used to steal his hoodies, too.

Shanaya realised that maybe this was what could help restore her and Sidharth's relationship. She knew Sidharth couldn't resist whenever she wore his clothes and it always ended up with him being too clingy to Shanaya. Desperate times calls for desperate measures and when nothing seemed to be right in their relationship, she knew this idea would definitely work. Another plan to commence after the cooking for him didn't work.

The next morning, Shanaya wore Sidharth's clothes and show it to him. She knew this wasn't the right way to bring back what seemed to have been lost, but she couldn't think of anything else.

Sidharth was in the shower when Shanaya put on the thrasher hoodie and wait for him outside. She knew Sidharth would leave all his work when he would see Shanaya wearing his hoodie.

When Sidharth came out of the shower just in his tracks and drying his hair. Shanaya tried to get his attention, but even though Sidharth looked at her, he didn't seem to react.

"Sidharth, don't you remember this hoodie?" Shanaya showed him what she's wearing shyly.

"Which hoodie, Sha?" Sidharth asked, looking at himself in the mirror.

"The one I'm wearing right now, look," Shanaya said, pointing at the hoodie.

"Not really... ah, isn't that one of my old hoodies? Where did you find it?" Sidharth asked nonchalantly.

"It's been in my closet for a long time and I found it yesterday while I was cleaning my closet." She replied sheepishly.

"Ah, that's why I couldn't find it the last time I was looking for it." Sidharth said, pulling over his black turtleneck.

"Do you want it? Then I can-"

"No need for it, Sha, it's fine. I don't even wear these types of hoodies anymore and it looks good on you, so you can keep it. By the way, I'm going out with Yoona tonight so I might be home late. Don't wait for me, yeah?" Saying that, Sidharth left.

Shanaya sat on the edge of their bed and stared blankly. She can't say that it didn't hurt when it did hurt so badly. She can feel her heart shatter from the disappointment and pain that Sidharth gave her. She didn't know what else to do. Maybe it was time, time to give Sidharth space and maybe, maybe by then, he'll notice their relationship slipping.

Shanaya thought of surprising Sidharth today, just for old times' sake. She missed having surprise dates with Sidharth and she wanted to have one even just at the dorm. But she never had the chance, since Sidharth was always in their dorm. She also thought that maybe Sidharth would find the gesture cute and show more affection to her.

"I'm gonna meet with my old high school friends. Do you wanna come?" Sidharth asked, looking at Shanaya.

"Nope, I gotta do some groceries." Shanaya leaned on the kitchen counter and took an apple.

"Oh, okay, I'll be back later." Sidharth responds, kind of surprised that Shanaya said no but just shrugged it off. Shanaya gave him a quick kiss on the cheek that the younger one of the two avoided. He opened the door and headed out.

Shanaya just smiled fakely at herself, and quickly changed her clothes and grabbed her things. She waited for 20 minutes to go by to make sure that Sidharth was already far away. This was the only opportunity he had to begin his surprise date.

Shanaya bought a cake, some groceries that she needed, and flowers. Then she began preparing for her surprise. Sidharth texted her he will be home late, which she replied with an "okay, take care baby" and she had more time to prepare now.

"Hm I should make some pasta? To make it romantic? What do you think, Ki?" Shanaya asked Kiya on the phone, as she washed the kitchen equipment that she'll use. She called Kiya to keep her company and ask about some of her opinions on which is better.

"You should. Pasta is the way!! Make it a candlelit dinner date," Kiya replied enthusiastically. The phone was on loudspeaker so she could start cooking.

"Okay, do scented candles work?" Shanaya chuckled.

"That's fine, you're boyfriend-girlfriend anyway," Kiya giggled on the other line. Shanaya smiled slightly at that.

"I'll hang up Kiyu, thank you!" Shanaya said.

"Anytime." Kiya replied and ended the call.

Shanaya looked at the time and saw that she still had 30 minutes to spare. She cooked the pasta and side dishes peacefully and texted Sidharth as if he's almost home.

"I'll be there in 10." Shanaya read his reply and rattled.

She didn't expect him to be home that fast. Shanaya moved quicker now and arranged the table set up with the flowers and candles on the table. She placed the sliced cake on separate plates for the two of them ahead and focused on the pasta. Luckily, everything was almost cooked, so she prepared the plates for them and slowly transferred them, placing it carefully on the table. Shanaya takes a last look at what she did, feeling proud of the outcome when she heard a knock on the door. She jumped at that but didn't dare open it until her phone rang. Sidharth was calling her. She turned off her phone immediately and turned off the lights with only the candles giving brightness. Shanaya hid herself behind the couch as she heard the door lock click.

"Sha? What's this?" Sidharth said as he saw the candles from afar and switched on the lights.

Shanaya emerged from behind the couch and said, "surprise!! Candlelit dinner date?"

"You prepared all this?" Sidharth asked, looking at the setup with the pasta and side dishes that Shanaya cooked.

"Yup, do you like it?" She looked at him with a bright smile, waiting for an answer.

"Thank you, Sha, this is amazing," Sidharth said and looked at her, "but I already ate and I'm full. I could keep you company, though."

"Oh," Shanaya's smile faltered, "it's okay!! You must be tired, you can rest!!"

"Okay, thank you," and with that, Sidharth left, changed his clothes, and lied on the bed.

Shanaya doesn't move and holds on to the chair for support. She sighs and smiles sadly at herself, looking at what she prepared. She wanted to eat them, but she lost her appetite and just wanted to curl in on herself and cry.

She just couldn't figure out what happened that changed them so much? What happened that changed Sidharth so much? It felt like they were having a whole different mind and vision for each other. Shanaya wanted to tell herself that all the choices and voices were all in her head, but sometimes Sidharth made her feel crazy and sometimes, like he hated her and damn, she hated that so much. She hated even the mere thought of it, but she was numb today. She just didn't know what was it and what wasn't anymore.

Shanaya decided to ignore Sidharth. Shanaya knew that if she starts doing this, she'll get hurt in the process as well. But if it was the only way to make Sidharth realise, then she will do it, for both of their sakes as well. She settled beside Sidharth, cuddling him for the last time before she would proceed with what she planned. The younger was already in a deep slumber and Shanaya's heart shattered piece by piece, slowly closing her eyes, taking him in once more.

Shanaya woke up to an empty bed without Sidharth again. It's been like this for the past few months, but it wasn't constant. There were times she would wake up first and plant a soft kiss on his cheek, trying not to wake him up. But this time, Shanaya thought that getting distant might be easier than he thought since Sidharth already was. She swallowed the lump forming in her throat at the thought that this will surely not end up well and she might lose Sidharth in the process. But she had to do this for the both of them, she'll try to save it in the way that she thinks would work.

Shanaya only wanted the best for Sidharth. She loved being there for him and doing everything together with him. Shanaya was the clingier one between the two of them and Sidharth loved that about her. He loved hearing her random I love you's, calling him by his pet name, and the kisses that he gets whenever he asks for them. But like every other relationship, it's never perfect. There are a lot of fights that happen as their relationship gets deeper, no more random I love you's and the kisses feel like a routine. The comfort and presence that they have with another are now enough.

But there are always times that Shanaya missed being Sidharth's baby. She missed the attention and endless love that Sidharth gave her. She's sure that the feelings are still there, but it's not the same. She needed assurance to comfort her insecurity about being the only one holding on to their relationship. There are times she gets clingy, but Sidharth just brushes her off like any other normal day. The I love you's that she tells him are replied with a nod and, at worst times, no reaction at all. Whenever she tried to ask for a kiss, she was just told, "I already gave you one." She doesn't even hear the pet name being used anymore. It maybe nothing to Sidharth, but those simple gestures of brushing Shanaya off did hurt her a lot. Some might say that she's just overreacting, but it's never the case when the one you're used to before was so different from what it is now.

Shanaya's eyes always glimmered whenever she saw Sidharth and she never fails to tell him the 3 words that she wants to express every day. But it's not the same for the other. That's when Shanaya realised that what people say is true; there's always someone that loves the other more in a relationship, and they're always the ones that get hurt more. Shanaya thinks that it's fine, though. As long as Sidharth is happy and he never feels the pain, then that's enough for her.

Shanaya moved her bed away from Sidharth's. When they started dating, they actually combined their beds to make it into a big one that they can share. Shanaya loved the idea the most and Sidharth was fine with it, saying that he could now move around more, too.

"Why are you moving your bed away?" Sidharth asked, his toothbrush in his hand, and looked at Shanaya.

"I want to sleep in my bed now." Shanaya replied coldly.

"Okay." Sidharth replied expressionless, and turned around to brush his teeth.

Shanaya bit her lower lip, already expecting that cold reply from Sidharth, but she still wasn't ready for it. It still hurt her.

"Did you cook breakfast?" She asked, wiping her mouth.

"Uh, no?" Sidharth replied.

"Okay, I'll probably just have bread, so if you want proper breakfast you can cook," Shanaya said and went inside the bathroom.

Shanaya doesn't know if what she's doing is right or wrong? Was it okay to ignore and distance herself from Sidharth like this? It just didn't feel right anymore. Something which was initially just to make Sidharth feel what she felt was turning out to distance them more than it had ever before. She had now started to hate her stupid game. She felt like she was losing him. Sidharth, whom she loved the most and who mattered the most to her.

Sidharth wasn't at all reacting to it, and it had now bugged her. Did he fall out of love? Has something happened? Was it something she did? Or simply was it just her?

She didn't know if she should continue this whole thing anymore, but she tried to ignore the negative thoughts and to do what she planned and not go against it. She wasn't letting her insecurities win over her trust in Sidharth; not this time.

Shanaya hasn't been sleeping that well since she stayed in her house more. She was mostly up at night overthinking things between Sidharth and her. She got used to Sidharth's scent all over the bed too, and it was now slowly fading away. She got up and headed to the kitchen, cooking her breakfast.

Shanaya was eating her breakfast when Sidharth woke up and walked over.

"We're making our own breakfasts again?" Sidharth asked, scratching the back of his head.

"I don't know, Sidharth, but what I made was only for one person." Shanaya emphasized on his name and bit on the boiled egg she's holding.

Sidharth, who was opening the fridge, was startled a bit upon hearing his name. He made it look like he didn't care and continued with what he was doing. Shanaya glanced at him and was disappointed to see Sidharth unfazed.

"What are you gonna do today, Sidharth?" Shanaya asked Sidharth, who was sitting across from her.

"There's no announcement for the next semester yet, so I'll play some games for now, I guess." He replied, taking a spoonful of rice.

"Okay, maybe I'll go to the university today to ask about mine." Shanaya said, trying to make a conversation. She doesn't know why she's still trying to when she has distanced herself.

"Alright."

"I will probably be back before lunch and I'll go with Ki." Shanaya continued talking.

"Send my regards to her." Sidharth said and stood up, bringing his empty plate to the sink and ending the conversation.

Shanaya clicks her tongue and cleans the table. She texts Kiya that she'll be there in 15 minutes and slips into a gray loose shirt.

"I'll be back." Shanaya leaves the dorm without looking at Sidharth and without giving him a kiss like she always does.

Sidharth noticed the change in Shanaya's attitude towards him but didn't say anything to the older. He thinks that his plan is finally working for Shanaya to treat him like this. At first, it killed Sidharth to see her sad, but eventually Shanaya seemed to be distancing herself from him. He honestly hates it, still but Shanaya's happiness comes first to him. If her hating Sidharth would make it easier on Shanaya and make her happy in the long run, then he was more than fine with being hated by the only person which mattered to him the most.

Shanaya meant a lot to Sidharth than he could even explain to anyone or himself. Sidharth didn't know why? Was it because no one has ever loved him like Shanaya did? or was it something else? But whatever it was, he was ready to go any lengths if Shanaya could be happy and if that meant she needed to hate him, then so be it.

She sat there on her desk with dim lights, a cup of coffee in her hand and her eyes staring at the moon. She kept thinking how different she used to be a few months back and what she has become now. There was a time she wanted to spend every moment with Sidharth, but now she was running away from each and every one of it. She just wanted to shower love at Sidharth, but didn't have the right to. But now, when she had the right, she was stopping herself from doing so. Ignoring Sidharth wasn't exactly as Shanaya expected it to be. It was hurting her more than she expected it would. She was doing it so that the younger would know how it felt to be on the receiving side, but Shanaya felt like this whole thing was back firing her. Sidharth was not reacting to any of it. In fact; he seemed to be pleased by it. Shanaya didn't know what hurt more, was it Shanaya trying to ignore Sidharth or was it Sidharth not being affected by it? Probably the latter.

At first Shanaya thought it was just some stupid mood swing of her boyfriend which had changed his attitude towards her, but as time passed, she realised that maybe it was not what she thought. Sidharth was intentionally being the way he was. Did he hate Shanaya now? Was she being too clingy? Did Sidharth want to break up? Shanaya knew she wouldn't be much surprised if that was the case because she considered herself to be someone who was hard to fall in love with.

She was stupid enough to think Sidharth would look at her any differently than others. After all, she made him feel different than others did. But of course Shanaya couldn't be loveable suddenly one day, right? Sidharth really must have tried his best, but alas, got tired of it. Everyone gets tired of Shanaya after all.

All those I love you's he said in return to Shanaya must have been fake because how can you get tired of someone you loved? Shanaya was sure she could never; She could never get tired of Sidharth. Not even if she wants to, but she can pretend if that's what Sidharth wanted. If he didn't want Shanaya anymore, then he shall have that. After all, Shanaya loves Sidharth more than she loves herself. She is ready to do so, but a part of her is selfish too. Selfish when it comes to Sidharth. So even for a little while she wants to do everything, she wants to do for Sidharth until she can't, until she won't and until it probably starts hurting less, but would it ever be that way was all Shanaya wondered about?

Sidharth was playing as usual while Shanaya was on her phone just scrolling through the internet when she received a text from Kiya. Sidharth glanced at her when her phone message notification sounded, but looked away just right after.

Shanaya suddenly stood up and walked towards her closet. Sidharth looked at her, but Shanaya was so focused on her phone that she didn't even spare him a glance. She changed her clothes, wore her sneakers, and tied them, saying nothing.

"You're going out?" Sidharth asked, staring at her.

"Yeah." Shanaya replied bitterly.

"With?"

"Kiya." She stood up and headed for the door.

"What time will you be back?" Sidharth avoids looking at her.

"I don't know." She got out and shut the door.

Sidharth turned around the moment the door closed. He could feel Shanaya being cold to him and he knows it's because of him. He heaves a deep sigh and leans back, telling himself that this is better and easier for him. If Shanaya was happier this way, then good, he won't interfere.

The next day, Sidharth woke up without Shanaya in the dorm. He wondered where the older was early in the morning when she returned late yesterday. Sidharth was gonna text Shanaya to ask her where she was when he spotted a note on the table.

"Be back by 12 -S"

Sidharth looked at the time and it was already 10 in the morning. He decided not to text Shanaya and just wait for her to arrive. He cooked brunch for himself and actually made more than for one person; Sidharth thought maybe Shanaya hadn't eaten lunch yet, so he let it be.

He was watching a movie when the door opened, revealing Shanaya. Shanaya just glanced at Sidharth, closed the door, and went to change her clothes.

"Where did you go?" Sidharth asked seriously.

"Somewhere."

"With?" He looked at Shanaya, who was already looking at him.

"No one." Shanaya replied nonchalantly.

"Have you eaten lunch? I cooked some for brunch." He says, looking away.

"Thanks, but I'm full." The older said with an awkward smile plastered on her face. She crashed into her bed and ignored Sidharth.

Shanaya woke up without Sidharth in the dorm. She felt emotionless, filled with thoughts about what she should do. She knows what she has to do, but she doesn't know if she wants to. Shanaya loves Sidharth too much. She always chose Sidharth more than herself, but she was already broken and she needed answers to help her decide.

Shanaya just stayed at home the whole time, staring into black space, thinking. Until Sidharth got home that afternoon and she looked at him.

"Sidharth, will you answer me truthfully if I ask you something?"

"Huh? Well, yeah, why would I lie to you," Sidharth replied, sitting down on the couch beside Shanaya with a space between them.

"Are you still happy being with me?" Shanaya looked at him, tears welling up in her eyes.

"What are you talking about?" The younger asked, looking away.

Shanaya already knew the answer, but she needed to hear it from him. She was hurting enough, and she didn't want both of them to get hurt more by being in this relationship.

She chokes back on her tears. "Stop playing dumb. Answer me honestly."

"Then stop asking me stupid questions." Sidharth got up to leave, but Shanaya grabbed his arm to look at him.

She took a deep breath. "I love you, Sidharth, but fuck you. You played me so hard. You sent me signals that you were interested. You talked to me all the time. You did everything that showed as if you loved me as well, but guess I was wrong, huh? And even though you never loved me, isn't it funny that the first thing that comes to my mind when someone says the word 'love' is 'you'? I think what hurts the most is the fact that I thought you felt the same - but you didn't," Shanaya scoffs. It's time to stop hurting. It's time to let go of this relationship.

"You know, there is a part of me that's desperate to know if my absence has done any damage to you. That there is a possibility that you too experience long restless nights due to the thought of me. That your heart is broken in the same way as mine. I want to know I'm not the only one hurting from this and that maybe even for once I meant something to you."

"I know I hurt you, even if I didn't intend to - it's just the way of love, isn't it? And it's sad because I couldn't see you struggle, so I did what I had to do. I did it because I care for you and even though I don't love you the same way, I do love you-" Shanaya swallowed the lump in her throat and looked at Sidharth, who avoided eye contact after speaking those words.

"You know what? I'm feeling hypnotized by the words that you just said. Don't lie to me, don't fucking lie to me, Sidharth. Try to just get in my head and you'll know how I feel. When the morning comes, you're still in my bed but it's so, so cold. I don't even know who you are anymore. You're not the one I fell in love with, Sidharth. Who the fuck are you because something has changed? You're not the same and I hate it. I'm sick of waiting for love, your love Sidharth. Every day I wake up thinking that you're just in a bad mood, but no, it's not just a one- day affair anymore. I just don't feel your love anymore. I feel like I lost you and when I say that, I'm not talking about my boyfriend only, but my fucking best friend, too." Shanaya continued talking.

"I still remember the way you cared about the little things I loved, the little things that hurt me. You gave me love, gave me friendship. And every time that you asked me what I want the most, I would say "just stay" and you said you will. If only you knew how much those little moments with you mattered to me." she gives off a small smile. Sidharth looked at her.

"You are my best friend, my first love, my priority, my everything. I have felt everything for you that I have never felt for anyone. I thought we were perfect for each other. The inseparable kind of lovers that the whole campus knew about, the 'you could never find Shanaya without Sidharth' and if you have to look for one, you'll be sure to find them with the other. I was sure that you're the one that I will have for my whole lifetime and everyone else was, too. I was happy with you. You're my safe place. I could share everything and anything that I wanted with you, and you were always there to listen. You were a call away when I needed you and I thought it would be like that until the end. And even though it is all still the same, why doesn't it fucking feel the same, Sidharth? What changed? Why did you fucking change Sidharth? because I'm pretty sure I didn't." She runs a hand through her hair and looked at the younger with tears in her eyes.

"You know sometimes I want to talk to you so bad but I feel like I'm bothering you or probably coming off clingy. I don't have anything particular to say, but I just want to talk to you. I don't know how to hold a conversation to save life, but I still want to talk to you. Even if you're breaking me bit by bit every day, I want to talk to you, spend time with you and want to live moments where I can love you because even though it's selfish, loving you is a way for me to love myself. I loved you the way I should have loved myself." Shanaya touched Sidharth's cheek lightly.

"But I think I have to let it all go. The way you kissed me, the way you smelled, the way you held my waist and pulled me in. I have to let you go. Because that's who you were and not who you are. I have to let you go, even though every moment with you was the happiest moment I have ever been. Falling in love with you was one of the most beautiful feelings and I would never wanna let this feeling go. But it's also true that it's high time I should fall in love with myself a little because I no longer feel comfortable being the Shanaya who loved herself through Sidharth. I want to be the

Shanaya who loves herself because she's special and not because Sidharth thinks she is. I have to let you go, not because you broke me, but because I let you break me, because I believed in something that wasn't real. You taught me a lot about love, even if you could not give it to me." Shanaya chuckles, smiling through his tears.

"Shanaya, you said a lot of things and that's totally justified, but what's worse is the fact that no one can understand the love I have for you, not even you." Sidharth said, holding Shanaya's hand.

Shanaya pulled her hand away. "I don't think I ever will, Sidharth. I want nothing but the best for you, I really do, it's just that sometimes I wish that the best for you was me. But to stop wishing that I need to leave you. I will never forget the moment I realised I loved you, but I think it's high time I start loving myself too." She leaned in to Sidharth, pressing her lips on his forehead, and left.

Sidharth stood still, clutching his chest, not expecting it to hurt that much even though he had wanted this. He felt warm tears streaming down his cheeks.

Wasn't this what he had wanted? Wasn't it him who wanted Shanaya to hate and eventually break up with him? Then why was it hurting so much? Why did he want to tell Shanaya his feelings and why he did what he did? Why could he feel his heart breaking into a million pieces and why did he feel like dying when he saw Shanaya crying? Why did it feel impossible to leave Shanaya when he wasn't really together with her in the first place?

He didn't know the answer to any of his questions, but what he knew was he didn't want all this anymore. He didn't want to hurt Shanaya. He didn't want Shanaya to hate him and he didn't want to break up. What he wanted was Shanaya and her belongingness towards him. What he wanted was for Shanaya to love him. What he wanted was his Shanaya even now when he couldn't have her—not anymore.

Shanaya and Sidharth just worked together. He doesn't know if it was love or just friendship, but they were partners in crime. Sidharth didn't know how or why, but she made him feel alive. Shanaya was the most beautiful person Sidharth had ever come across. She was the one who would drag him to the park at night just to sit on the swings and listen to their favourite music and not care what others thought of them seeing them swinging like some kids. She was the one who would ask him to drive them somewhere they haven't been before, just so that Sidharth could click some beautiful pictures because she knew the younger loved clicking pictures and she loved Sidharth. Being with Shanaya made him so happy and he didn't even realise how, but it did.

But Shanaya deserved someone who loved her with every single beat of his heart, someone who constantly keeps thinking about her. She needs someone who treats her with respect and prioritizes her happiness over everything else. Shanaya deserves someone who can make her happy and make her feel loved and important and all the best things in the world. To whom Shanaya would be nothing less than their entire world because to Sidharth — Shanaya and her happiness were his entire world.

Sidharth woke up without Shanaya in sight. He assumed she must already be at school and got up. He checked the time on his phone and realised that it was a Sunday and Shanaya usually sleeps in during this time. Sidharth turned to see Shanaya's bed empty and organized, like no one slept there the night before, and noticed something odd. Shanaya's things weren't there anymore.

Panic started to rise in his body and he rushed to the living room, but there was no Shanaya anywhere. He could only hear his heart beating wildly and the clock ticking. Shanaya was gone.

He ran a hand through his hair and got himself a glass of water as he sat down on the couch in the living room. Sidharth was so lost. He didn't know what to do and where he should find Shanaya, or did she even want to be found? He heaved a deep sigh and hung his head low when he noticed a paper on the coffee table.

"To Sidharth. To me??!?" Sidharth said as he read the back of the letter and flipped it open.

"Hey Sidharth, by the time you read this letter, I have already left this place for good. I wasn't going to say anything and just leave, but I thought that you at least deserve an apology from me. I know it was partially my fault that our relationship came to that point. I was too selfish and too blind to see that you were never happy with me. I'm sorry for taking away the peace in your life just to satisfy my desire to be with you and for assuming things straight ahead without thinking about it. I won't say I didn't notice you being distant and uncomfortable within the last weeks of our relationship because I did and just brushed it off. It did hurt a lot, but I thought that it would hurt more if you left without thinking that I was already being selfish. I never expected that we would actually end up together and have all this break up thing. I genuinely loved you as my best friend and as my lover. You made me so happy beyond words, and it felt like I was the luckiest girl alive to be loved by you. You've helped me grow into someone better and always prioritized my feelings before yours, and I'm thankful for that. You gave me the happiest days I've had in my life and for that I'm glad I met you despite the hurt that you gave in the end. But no matter how much I try to hate you, I just couldn't bring myself to. I love you too much and I will always want what's best for you. Our chapter has ended Sid, thank you for being with me. I hope you'll find someone that would make you happy just by their presence, turn your frown into a smile in just a snap, your exhausting days into bearable ones, love you more than you love them and make you feel the way you made me feel with just your existence. I'm letting you go. Thank you for everything. I once loved you, Sidharth, and maybe you'll always be in my heart. Take care always. Love, Shanaya"

"No.. no.. Sha.. this can't be real." Sidharth clutched the letter in his hands, bringing it to his chest. He could feel his heart break over and over again. He lost Shanaya and this time, it was real. There was no turning back and nowhere to find his best friend ever again. His best friend who had been with him ever since. The one who would always come running whenever he needed someone. Shanaya, who only cherished him with every second that passed by, was gone from his life. He didn't know what to do. Sidharth just stared blankly at the wall as tears streamed down his face. He touched the tears on his cheeks and smiled bitterly to himself. He didn't even realize he was already crying.

"Sha, I'm sorry. I'm so, so, sorry..."

Sidharth knew that there was nothing else that he could do and he fucked everything up. If only he could've loved Shanaya as much as she loved him. If only he knew it would turn out like this, he could have prevented all of it from happening. But it was already too late, and he lost Shanaya. He lost the person who meant the most to him; he lost his best friend; he lost the only person who would love him that much. How could he be so stupid? How could he hurt her that much? Sidharth breaks down once again, knowing that nothing will ever be the same again.

Shanaya changed her college because she wasn't able to handle all those faces mocking her, even saying nothing. All she could think was how miserable everyone must be thinking of her to be. A girl who fell in love with a friend of hers, all the while being unable to see his actual intentions. A girl who lost herself in the path of loving someone she deeply cared about.

These emotions stayed with her for a long time. Shanaya always wondered if time will really help her heal wounds she thinks are too deeply rooted within her. And much to her surprise, it did exactly what it was supposed to do. Such a funny thing Time is. It makes you think that whatever you don't have is worth getting, only to realize that the time you spent on getting it would have been useful in some other activity.

It has been 15 years since that unfortunate incident with Sidharth and Shanaya was now the holder of the Photographer of The Year award and that too for a record 3 times in a row which takes her to the list of people who could achieve this feat with sheer willpower and let's say some lucky shots and angles. She was happy. Her family was happy and the person who helped her through the gloomy phase of depression is ever so cheerful for her.....Kiya. She helped her to make this dream come true and, like Shanaya, she too is into wildlife photography. Taking tips from her senior as usual.

But the one person who was standing like a pillar behind Shanaya all this time was Varun. He was the CEO of a media house. The human heart is such a unique thing. If you loved someone dearly and after some conflict you decide to be apart, it still searches for someone who is like the previous individual. Just that now it wants all those bad habits to be removed and all the good ones to be in them. Varun was all that she could hope for. Varun supported her when she felt lost and broken. He was the one who gave her an opportunity to grow and become the person she was today. He was sweet, charming and always showed her he loved her, but never asked her for anything in return. Just selflessly loving her and helping her become a better person. Encouraging her and never failing to remind her how special she was, just not in herself but also to him. Shanaya never realized when this friendship turned into love, but it all felt so natural. As natural as it is for a tree to grow from a seed and for the sun to rise after a night. On the journey to love herself, she found someone who loved her for her.

Who says one falls in love when you actually grow in it? Just like Shanaya did. Varun's love strengthened her and a better version of herself. She wasn't co- dependent on him but his presence just made everything so much better—so much worthwhile.

Varun just didn't make her happy, but also brought out the happiest versions of her from within of her. He helped her embrace everything she didn't even know she already had in her. The things she had always tried to find in others were already in her. It just needed the right person for it to bloom, and Varun was that right person for Shanaya. Shanaya couldn't have been happier than she was now.

And what about Sidharth?? What scientists have learnt about human emotions. It takes a pretty heavy toll on someone whose intention was to do something good, but it went pretty badly. And Sid was no exception. He felt hugely at fault for Shanaya being so insecure. The poor girl just wanted his love, which he gave her or at least pretended to give.

One day they met. Shanaya was the one who diverted his attention to herself since he was engaged in some other activity. They met on a street on a lovely moonlit night. She was the first to speak. "Heyy Sid!! How long has it been since we met?? You look different. In a good way, obviously. Also, we should meet often, just for the old times' sake. I will let Kiya know you didn't go AWOL after our unfortunate incident. Also, I'm with Varun now. U might not know him since he isn't from around here, but I think you will like him since you two have a lot in common starting with the love of sports."

Sidharth was feeling broken after hearing that she has been with a guy since she left college. It was probably one of those feelings you get when you cheat with someone and still want to claim them. One can feel whatever they want to, but when you decide to cross a certain threshold, it gets way past telling them you actually meant it for their good.

"Oh, uh…. I wasn't actually AWOL. I was just busy with my life. But anyway, now that we have met, I was thinking of a reunion kind of thing. You, me and Kiya. And uh Shanaya, is there any chance that you forgive me after all these years?" said Siddharth.

Shanaya was smiling gently. She had already forgiven him a long time back when she realized he helped her to realize her worth and, though the outcome was unfortunate, his intentions were pure. She said, "Now, don't be so formal, dude. You were quite good, in a way. Yes, you were rude to me, but it was just a bad way to implement something good. I realized that a long time ago and it will be well that you do too. Don't live with this guilt. It will lead you nowhere"

They got on good terms at the end. Kiya later met with Siddharth, and just like her friend Shanaya, she was sweet to him. It is a good thing that they were now a merry trio again. The line Sidharth made between them was always a little fuzzy, but still visible, and now there were no more flirty exchanges. But at least it was a better beginning than how it ended in college.

Nikhil and Shalini were about to get married. They have been in a loving relationship for a long time and it was time for them to hold hands for their entire lives. Strange how some people just find a person and decide to stay with them. The love that is present in the environment between those two individuals is something that everyone craves. They are just afraid to ask for it.

Sidharth, Shanaya and Kiya attended the wedding and Nikhil bhaiya was in tears when the latter saw the trio. It was like a memory coming to life for him. He was happy for his friend getting the closure that he so much craved. After all, he knew that the ones who hurt others have gone on a guilt trip. Fortunate are the ones who return from it after becoming strong, both emotionally and mentally. Just like Sidharth here.

Shanaya was her usual self now. From being a shy girl who wasn't able to confess her feelings to her friend to being this independent woman who is living the life she wanted when she was a child, she came all the way to her home. She found her love Varun, her friend who thought that she never forgave him, and Kiya was always there to support her through her worst of times to cheer her when she was on the stage to get the award.

***